Mystic

THE COTTAGE

Prequel to the

MYSTIC VALLEY
SERIES

Mystic Valley series

The Cottage

This book is sold subject to the condition that it shall not, by way of trade or otherwise, be lent, re-sold, duplicated, hired out, or otherwise circulated without the publisher's prior written consent, in any form of binding or cover other than that in which it is published and without similar condition, including this condition, being imposed on the subsequent purchaser.

Text Copyright © 2016 Lavinia Urban

All rights reserved

Mystic Valley series

Disclaimer

This is a work of fiction. All characters and events portrayed in this novel are fictitious and are products of the author's imagination. Any resemblance to actual events, or locales or persons, living or dead are entirely coincidental.

Cover by: Magen McMinimy

Edited by: Joyce Wetherbee

**ISBN-13:
978-1542891196**

**ISBN-10:
1542891191**

Mystic Valley series

Chapter One

If you had asked Lydia Green, six months ago, how her life was she would tell you it was perfect. She had just been promoted to Senior Marketing Executive in a soft drinks company. Her marriage to Steve was perfect, even though they now had to put trying for a baby on the back burner for a while, considering her workload was about to increase.

Lydia had met Steve at University, where they had both been studying for a business degree. Steve was a charmer. Lydia initially had no interest in dating, choosing to focus on getting her degree, but Steve was relentless and went out of his way to get that first date, even roping in the help of her best friend Mandy.

Lydia stood five foot five with an unruly mass of brown hair that mainly stayed a frizzy mess. Lydia did not have time for a beauty regime and she could never understand why Steve had been attracted to her. He always said it was her eyes, which were the deepest emerald green anyone had ever seen. It was always the first thing people saw and the one thing they remembered about her.

Whereas Lydia studied, Steve partied, which was one of the main reasons he dropped out and instead became an Estate Agent.

Steve stood a little over six foot with a wiry frame, dirty blonde hair and brown eyes. He was definitely attractive and could have had the pick of any girl, but he had chosen Lydia and now five years on they were happily married and living in an apartment in central London. A luxury apartment secured by Steve's connection in the realty world.

As Lydia's workload increased she spent more time at the office and less time with Steve, who constantly reassured her that he completely understood. Lydia was too distracted to think otherwise.

It was Thursday morning and Lydia was up to her eyeballs in work. There were two days until the project was supposed to be completed then aired on T.V. and the actress they planned on using in the advert had been involved in a scandal that was all over the papers. Now the company's directors did not want her face associated with their campaign.

Talk about cutting it close. Most people would have said it was impossible and Lydia had been close to saying those same words. But her determination for perfection had taken over and now she was barking orders into the phone whilst filtering through paperwork, both physical and virtual.

Tunnel vision had kicked in, so much so that she hadn't heard a knock on her office door. It wasn't until her secretary, Audrey, stepped in and closed the door.

Audrey was in her late sixties and past the age of retirement but she chose to work and the company wanted to keep her because she was good at her job. Over the years Lydia came to think of Audrey as irreplaceable.

She stood a little over five foot seven with grey hair that was always pulled back and twisted at the back of her head. She wore glasses, but not always on her face. Most of the time they hung around her neck on a black and red gemmed chain.

Her build was slim with an overly large chest that made Lydia often jokingly question how her buttons didn't pop open on her blouses. Audrey always gave a smile and a wink and said it was down to years and years of practice.

The majority of the time Audrey wore a blank expression, giving nothing away. It was only with Lydia that true emotions played on her face.

As Lydia looked up she saw the worried expression which Audrey was trying to mask as she leant back on the door whilst waiting for Lydia to finish her phone call.

Choosing not to let Audrey's face or presence distract her, Lydia turned away, after holding up one finger.

Audrey waited patiently as Lydia barked orders that she wanted things done as of yesterday.

With a huge sigh, Lydia finally hung up the phone and turned to raise her eyebrows in Audrey's direction.

"There's a policeman and a solicitor here to see you."

Lydia rolled her head back and closed her eyes. She was convinced that the actress was trying to ensure that she still got paid. She probably had some court order.

"They need to speak to someone in the legal department." Lydia groaned without opening her eyes.

When Audrey didn't respond Lydia opened one eye and stared at her.

Audrey wringed her hands and looked everywhere but to Lydia, making Lydia annoyed.

Opening both eyes, she sat forward and put her hands on the table.

"Out with it."

"There here to see you." Audrey's eyes nervously met Lydia's. "It's about your parents."

Lydia's eyes grew wide.

"My parents?"

Audrey nodded.

Lydia hadn't seen her parents since she left for University. There were no phone calls, letters, nothing. They hadn't even come to her wedding. The problem was, Lydia didn't really remember them. It was as though all memories before University were hazy. She had always put it down to the fact that maybe she had fallen out with them. That could be the only explanation. She knew she had parents and she felt as though they loved her deeply and she them. That's all that mattered.

Lydia had never questioned it. She never sought them out.

On the couple of occasions when Steve and Amanda had probed her about her childhood or her parents Lydia had tried to recall a memory, any memory, but every time she did she felt a sharp pain in her head. It had got to the stage where people had just stopped asking her. They never once believed that she couldn't remember.

"You best send them in." Lydia's voice turning almost robotic as though something else had taken over her body.

Without another word Audrey slipped outside only to return seconds later with both the policeman and the solicitor.

On first impression Lydia stifled a laugh. It was her nerves and it didn't help that the policeman stood around six foot six, slim and impeccably dressed in his uniform. The solicitor was the complete opposite. He stood a little over four foot, stocky, wearing a brown suit and holding a suitcase almost half the size of him.

The two of them together looked to have stepped straight out of a comedy sketch.

As the two stepped into the room, the policeman took off his hat and nodded to Audrey as she pulled the door closed as she left.

The professional side of Lydia took over as soon as that door clicked making her spring to her feet and wave a hand in front of her.

"Gentlemen." She smiled. "Won't you take a seat."

In front of her desk were two chairs and the solicitor quickly moved to climb into it as both Lydia and the policemen watched on. Lydia was going to offer him some assistance but she was sure it would be rude of her to do so, so instead she remained quiet.

It was only when they were both seated that Lydia finally sat down, feeling nerves almost taking complete control of her body.

"How may I help you?" Lydia gave a fake smile. She felt that she knew what was coming before the policeman started talking.

"I am very sorry to inform you, but there has been an accident." He started.

Lydia zoned out, only catching fragments of what he was saying.

Something about a car accident and dead on impact.

It wasn't until the solicitor starting coughing loudly, trying to get Lydia's attention, that she realised that the policeman had finished and the solicitor had opened his briefcase.

Lydia, in almost a trance-like state, moved her eyes from the policeman to the solicitor and then the piece of paper he held in his hands.

"Sorry." Lydia blinked. "Please continue."

"I know it is a lot to take in but your parents left everything to you, which includes their cottage in Mystic Valley and all of the surrounding land." He paused, making sure Lydia was paying attention. Happy that she was he pulled a few other things from his briefcase, closed it then pushed it to the floor with a thump. Only then did he climb down from his chair and step onto the briefcase.

Neither Lydia nor the policeman said anything as the solicitor placed a folder on her desk as well as a set of keys.

"In there," he pressed a stubby finger on top of the folder, "is all the paperwork you will need. It includes the deeds."

"Is there an address?" Lydia hadn't realised she had spoken until she saw the odd look from the policeman.

The solicitor, however, looked unfazed.

Mystic Valley series

The policeman was wondering how she did not know the address to her family home. The home she had grown up in.

Lydia wondered this too.

"Everything is all in there." He emphasised the word 'everything' as though it had some hidden meaning.

Chapter Two

Everything around Lydia seemed to speed up as she sat there in a daze.

The policeman and solicitor left. Audrey came into her room, several times. All the while Lydia just sat there taking nothing in.

She felt like a snail in a sports car race.

One of the company Directors, Mr Montgomery, came in. He was shouting the odds but all he sounded like was an annoying wasp too close to her ear and begging to be swatted.

After Mr Montgomery, a tall, lean, greying man in his fifties, had almost worn a hole in the carpet, Lydia stood. In that moment, as she reached for her bag before reaching for the folder and set of keys that the solicitor had left, everything slowed down to normal speed and Mr Montgomery stopped in front of her desk and stared at her.

"Where do you think you're going?" He demanded.

"Home." Lydia muttered, feeling drained.

Mr Montgomery blanched. His face turned red and he looked as though he were going to get an aneurysm. "You can't go home. We're in the middle of a crisis. We have less than forty-eight hours to make a new advert."

For once, Lydia didn't care.

"You'll have to find someone else." She shrugged.

This resulted in Mr Montgomery turning almost purple. At that moment Audrey happened to step into the room. She'd been back and forth since Mr Montgomery arrived, asking if either of them needed anything.

"Audrey can help." To which Audrey looked confused and Mr Montgomery looked at Lydia as though she'd lost her mind. "Audrey has been with this company from the start. She knows my job and my accounts like the back of her hand."

"What you are suggesting is totally absurd." Mr Montgomery flustered.

Lydia moved to where her coat hung and folded it over her arm before sighing as she turned back to Mr Montgomery.

She could have stayed there arguing. Defending her suggestion but Lydia felt numb.

Finally, she shrugged. "Fine. Whatever. I'm going home."

Without even waiting for a response Lydia left.

***

Lydia's apartment building was over five floors - ground floor right through to fourth. Every floor had two apartments except the fourth which covered the entire floor and had access to the roof. This was Lydia and Steve's apartment and they loved it. In the summer months they would sit on the roof and admire the skyline with a bottle of wine. It was their own little sanctuary.

Walking into the building, Lydia chose to climb the stairs instead of taking the lift. She wanted time to think. Think about her parents. Parents who... no matter how hard she tried she couldn't remember.

Yes, she remembered their faces but that was only because she kept a box with their picture in it along with some little trinket that Lydia could not decide if it was made from metal or rock. She had no idea what it was for but she knew it was for something important and she needed to protect it. Why? Who knows.

When Lydia finally made it into her apartment she lay the folder and keys that the solicitor had given her, down on the end table next to the front door before dropping her coat on the back of the sofa and dumping her handbag on the floor.

As if on autopilot, Lydia made her way to her bedroom and straight to her underwear drawer where she kept the box with the picture of her parents and the trinket. Lydia rarely took it out and she'd never shown anyone what was inside. Not even Steve.

Sitting on her bed Lydia lifted out the small picture of her parents. She couldn't recall when it was taken but they looked to be in their early forties. Her father's hair was mainly grey with a few dark hairs blended in. His eyes, which were grey, seemed to twinkle.

Her mother had long dark hair with a dusting of grey. Her eyes were a deep emerald green, the same colour as Lydia's.

For the most part, Lydia could pass as the younger sister of her mums. The only difference was her chin. A chin which matched her father's, right down to the dimple in the middle.

Tears welled in Lydia's eyes. More for the fact that she couldn't remember anything about them. All she had was this picture of them both smiling widely.

A thump from above jolted Lydia from her thoughts. Putting the picture back in the box before hiding it back in her underwear drawer, Lydia moved to the stairs that led to the roof.

Pausing, Lydia strained her ears until she heard the sound of voices. One of them definitely Steve's which Lydia thought was odd as he was supposed to be at work.

As quietly as she could Lydia slowly ascended the stairs until her head peaked through the door.

The hot tub was on and Lydia could see the back of Steve's head. He was saying something she couldn't distinguish and Lydia wasn't sure to who because she couldn't see anyone, then she heard a laugh. A laugh she knew all too well. It belonged to her best friend Mandy.

A part of Lydia wanted to believe that it was merely platonic why she was here in the hot tub alone with her husband but then Steve moved to the other side of the hot tub and Lydia watched as Mandy's arms slid around his neck and her fingers tangled in Steve's hair as she pulled him down for a kiss.

Lydia covered her mouth and moved back. Tears welled in her eyes. Her stomach twisted. She felt physically sick. How could they? How long had it been going on? Question after question spun around Lydia's head as she almost stumbled down the stairs.

Mystic Valley series

In the hot tub Steve and Mandy looked around at the noise but saw nothing.

"Do you think Lydia's back early?" Mandy asked but Steve shook his head.

"Definitely not." He chuckled. "She probably won't be back until near midnight." He told her as he began to pull off Mandy's bikini bottoms. Steve was already completely naked.

"True." Mandy agreed with a smile as Steve pushed inside her.

Downstairs Lydia hurried to her bedroom and pulled out two suitcases and began filling them with all her possessions, which wasn't a lot.

A small part of her wanted to confront them. Show them that they'd been caught in the act but Lydia didn't want the drama. She didn't want to argue. She just needed to get out of here.

Once packed Lydia moved the suitcases to the front door. It was only when she went to retrieve her coat that she saw Steve's clothes lying on the floor besides the sofa.

Inwardly she cursed herself for not noticing sooner.

On the coffee table she also noticed his wallet and his car keys to his precious black Range Rover sport. On impulse she reached for them both, putting the keys in her pocket before opening the wallet.

Inside were two credit cards as well as cash. One of the credit cards was Steve's personal one. The one his wages got paid into. The other one was for the joint bank account which so happened to be the one her wages got paid into.

Through her tears Lydia snorted. She should have known. Lydia paid for everything. The car, this apartment, the bills. Everything came out of her wages. Lydia never once batted an eye because she got paid nearly five times as much as Steve.

Pulling out this card she put it in her back pocket. But before she closed it she spotted her wedding ring. Angry, Lydia pulled it off and placed it inside Steve's wallet before tossing it back onto the table.

Without looking back Lydia walked out of the front door.

Chapter Three

After clearing out the joint bank account Lydia got back in the car and just started driving. It wasn't until she had been driving for a few hours that she saw a sign for Manchester. It was only then that she realized that sub-consciously she knew exactly where she was heading. Home

Lydia may not recall where home was but after a brief stop at one of the motorway service stations and pulling out the folder she got from the solicitor she knew it was the only place to go.

For fifteen minutes Lydia had tried to put the address in the car's Satnav but she kept getting an error message that said 'Destination unknown.'

After slumping forward and resting her head on the steering wheel, Lydia decided to just keep driving and hope for the best. If it got dark she would find a hotel for the night.

After almost ten hours of driving the sky was blanketed in black with twinkling stars when Lydia passed a cottage with a lit lantern on the porch. Something about the cottage seemed familiar. She didn't know what. There were no memories that she could recall with the image of that cottage but there was definitely something familiar about it.

As Lydia continued to drive she had to go slower as the roads became narrower and windier. After almost an hour she slowed the car to a crawl.

It was odd but she could feel the cottage before she even saw it. Slowly she turned right into a long winding driveway before pulling outside her parent's cottage that looked eerie as it sat there in the dark surrounded by high bushes, trees and flowers.

Switching off the car Lydia just sat there staring. Up until this point she had no recollection of the cottage and still didn't, but if someone had given her pictures of a hundred different homes she would know this was her family home.

It was a simple two floored cottage made from large rocks. But where most homes looked warm and welcoming this one looked sad and gloomy. To some, even scary. To Lydia, she felt warmth but also the sadness. Sadness of knowing that her parents were not inside.

Lydia had no idea how long she had sat there staring. It wasn't until a crow cawed that caused Lydia to scream and jump.

Giving herself a mental telling off for being so fearful about going inside, Lydia reached over to grab the keys and folder as well as her handbag before climbing out of the car and walking towards the front door.

The set of keys were simple. There were two of them – front and back door.

The front door creaked as it opened and for a few moments Lydia just stood there.

"Hello?" She called out, knowing that no one would answer.

Pulling her phone from her handbag she turned on her torch and stepped inside in search of a light switch. Finally, she found one after almost ten minutes of looking. Someone had had the crazy idea to put it as far away from the front door as possible.

Lydia stood in a narrow hallway that had scenic pictures hung along one wall and a staircase at the other. At the opposite end from the front door was a small bathroom. Lydia knew this because the light switch was right next to it and when she had turned it on she had peaked inside to see a toilet, sink and a bath in a cramped tiny room. There wasn't enough space to swing a cat. The door to the bathroom didn't even open all the way as it hit against the toilet.

To the right of the front door was a kitchen with a circular table in the centre with three chairs. Lydia wondered if one of those chairs was hers. Had she sat there for meals with her parents?

To the left of the front door was a small lounge with a large fire place with a three-seater sofa and two armchairs surrounding it. On the back of the sofa lay a large blanket, which made Lydia reach out to run her fingertips across it. As she did, she continued to look around and noticed that against two of the walls there stood floor to ceiling bookcases, jam packed full of books that looked to be older than Lydia.

As Lydia's eyes skimmed the books she moved to the sofa. On autopilot reached to pull the blanket to wrap around herself.

A familiar smell lingered in the material as warmth spread throughout making her eyes grow heavy as she adjusted herself on the sofa before falling into a deep sleep.

***

Lydia dreamt that she was walking barefooted through a forest. It was the middle of the day and the sun shone from high above, penetrating through the trees branches and casting shadows on the forest floor.

She wore a long flowing pale green dress with a plunging neckline. Her hair, which was normally tied in a French chignon was loose and flowing freely down her back in waves.

All around her the sounds of the wildlife could be heard.

Lydia smiled with a blissful sigh. She'd never felt so happy and content.

As she moved through the trees, stopping every so often to observe different creatures, Lydia heard a splash coming from the river. She expected it to be an otter or duck but as she moved closer she realised it was a man.

Being careful, so as not to be seen, Lydia hid behind a tree but peeking out to observe the man.

Who was he? Why was he here? No one ever came here. This had always been her sanctuary.

Lydia watched as the man swam to the edge before pulling himself out.

He stood a little over six foot with defined muscles from head to toe. Lydia had to bite her bottom lip when she discovered that the man was completely naked. She had never seen a man like this. He made her heart race as she struggled to move her eyes back to his face where he pulled at his wet, jaw length dark hair before tying it at the back of his head. Not all of his hair obeyed and Lydia watched a few strands fall forward into his face. So badly did Lydia want to step forward, reach up and tuck them behind his ears before trailing her fingertips all over his body.

She sighed. Louder than she had wanted as the man looked around and within seconds his dark blue eyes pierced her.

Lydia gasped and tumbled backwards.

***

"Ouch." Lydia rubbed her head as she looked around wondering where she was.

It took a few moments before she remembered she was in the cottage.

Daylight was streaming in through the windows as Lydia lay in a tangled mess on the stone floor of the living room.

She recalled the dream that had seemed so real. Real enough that she did fall but off the sofa and hitting her head on the stoned floor in the process.

Untangling herself from the blanket Lydia made her way to the kitchen where she hoped there would be coffee. Inwardly, she cheered as she spotted a fancy coffee machine with a rack full of coffee pods.

After choosing a flavour, Lydia turned on the machine before quickly grabbing her phone.

Fifteen missed calls and seven text messages all of which were from Steve.

Dread, fear, and apprehension took hold as she slowly began reading the messages but by the end she was angry. It was as though he hadn't noticed she'd gone. He was asking if she had seen his car when she got home the night before or if it was there when she had left for work. More saying that he'd called the police because it looks like it'd been stolen.

Lydia wanted to reply and give him a mouthful even if to tell him that she had the stupid car. It was technically hers. She'd paid for it. Everything was in her name.

By the sound of it he hadn't noticed her wedding ring or the credit card missing and he'd definitely not noticed that all her clothes were gone. It made her wonder how long had it been since he really stopped noticing her existence at all. If the car was there, how long would it have been before he had even texted or called?

Lydia didn't want to think about it or even be tempted to respond to him, so instead she chose to turn her phone off. And after three cups of coffee she was ready to explore the cottage.

After placing her cup in the sink Lydia made her way upstairs. The first thing she noticed was how this level seemed to be made from wood. It was as though when the cottage was originally created it was only meant to be one floor. This level had more of a warm and homely feel. The walls were decorated in pale lemon wallpaper and on the walls were family pictures.

There were lots of Lydia and most were when she was a young child.

As she looked at each and every picture all of which had happy, smiley faces it made Lydia confused. If she was so happy then why couldn't she remember it and why had she been living in London.

As Lydia continued to look at the pictures there were unfamiliar faces amongst those of her and her parents. Then she saw him. The man from her dreams. He looked younger but there was no denying that it was him. To make matters even more confusing there were a lot of the two of them together. Were they friends? Or even more than that? Was he the reason she left?

As she moved around the landing, looking from picture to picture, Lydia came to a door. There were two doors, both of them closed, and as her hand hovered over the door handle she got a strange sense that this was her parents bedroom. She could turn the handle, step inside in a hope to discover more about her parents. Maybe even more about herself.

Quickly she dropped her hand.

She wasn't ready.

Not yet.

Turning around and with her back towards her parents' bedroom, Lydia looked straight ahead at a large brown door.

Taking a deep breath Lydia took two long strides towards it. Without hesitation she grabbed the handle and opened the door.

Lydia had hoped that opening this door would bring back memories. Yes, she knew it was her bedroom even though she remembered nothing.

In the centre of the room sat a wooden double bed with flower lights entwined in her headboard. The bedspread was covered in flowers. The floor was carpeted thick and green. The ceiling was a mixture of blue and white. When Lydia looked closely she saw that it looked a lot like a blue sky with clouds.

With the theme her walls were painted to look like a forest but as Lydia moved around the room she spotted fairies mixed in with the wildlife that were painted on her walls. Some happily flew around the trees and others peeked around tree trunks. Whoever had painted this room was truly gifted.

Apart from the bed there was a wardrobe, chest of drawers, vanity table and two bedside tables.

Lydia wondered when she had last been here. The room looked so clean as though it were more of a show room.

To her surprise, when she opened her wardrobe she'd expected to find clothes that were too small for her. Clothes for a child. But everything in here was all in her size. Not only that they were completely different to what she'd normally wear. So many dresses in so many flamboyant colours.

Lydia gasped.

Right at the end hung a green dress. The same green dress from her dreams. Instantly she pulled it out thinking that her eyes were deceiving her but it was the exact same dress.

How was this even possible?

Without even thinking Lydia began to change into it. It fit her perfectly.

On the back of the bedroom door hung a mirror. Standing in front of it Lydia released her hair, which was still tied up from yesterday and a bit messy from sleep. But after she ran her fingers through it she made it look somewhat presentable.

All she could do was just stare at herself in the mirror with her mouth open wide.

She would have stayed like that for hours but just then the sound of a bell ringing could be heard. Lydia had no idea what it was or where it was coming from except that it came from downstairs.

Hurrying out of the room, Lydia almost ran down the stairs. She was just about to go into the kitchen when the bell could be heard again.

It came from the front door and through the glass, at the top of the door, Lydia could see a tall figure.

She wondered who it could be. Maybe a neighbour? The only home she had seen, besides this was that cottage she passed but that was almost a half hours drive away.

It could be friends of her parents. She was sure it was no one she knew because no one had any idea she was here. She hadn't realised she was coming here herself.

When she opened the door she saw a man. His back was turned as though he were about to leave but the sound of the door opening had him turning around.

Lydia gasped and almost fell backwards. This time the man caught her.

"It's you." Lydia shook her head as the man held her arms to stop her from falling. She was transfixed in those big blue eyes.

"You remember me?" He sounded surprised.

For a moment Lydia was dumbfounded. The giddiness at seeing him had messed with her brain cells and it took a few minutes before she pulled back some type of common sense.

Mystic Valley series

How could they possibly have had the same dream? She didn't want to tell him that she had seen him in her dreams because she would sound like a complete moron.

"The pictures." She suddenly stammered, remembering all of the photographs hanging on the walls.

Before Lydia had spoken there had been hope in the man's eyes but that quickly disappeared, only to be replaced by sadness.

"Having a reunion party without me?" A female voice chirped causing Lydia's head to whip in the direction of the voice as a woman, in her early twenties, breezed past and into the house.

Lydia watched in both intrigue and surprise at the woman's rudeness as she went straight into the kitchen and opened the fridge.

The woman sighed at the empty fridge and shook her head before closing it. "How can we have a reunion without drinks?" She rolled her eyes in Lydia's direction.

She stood around five foot four with dark hair to her shoulders which she tucked behind her ears. Her eyes, which were a deep blue, were emphasised by dark eye make up. She wore dark jeans with heavy, black boots that stopped mid-calf and a dark t-shirt with red writing that read 'Lick Me.'

Classy, Lydia sarcastically thought but something about the woman had her mesmerised. She fascinated Lydia and she also felt familiar. Had she been in one of the pictures upstairs?

Just then the woman wiggled her eyebrows before turning back to the fridge.

"Kim. Don't." The man called out but it was too late. The woman that Lydia now knew as Kim opened the fridge door but instead of being empty it was now full.

"Chill ya beans, Lucas." Kim rolled her eyes before pulling out three bottles and preceding to use her teeth to take the lids off. "Here." She stepped forward and handed both Lydia and Lucas a cold bottle of cider before pulling out a chair at the kitchen table and sitting down.

Lucas sighed and shook his head.

Lydia just stood there looking at the bottle in disbelief. What had just happened? The fridge was empty. When she finally did look up, Kim had a large smile on her face. She knew she had surprised and confused Lydia and it was amusing to see Lydia's reaction.

"Not cool." Lucas sighed as he walked past Lydia to join Kim at the table. All the while Lydia was wondering what was going on and who were these people.

"Hey," Kim shrugged. "I'm just trying to help her memories come back." She proclaimed to Lucas before quickly turning back to Lydia. "They haven't come back yet, have they?" She raised an eyebrow as Lydia stood there with a bottle in hand whilst opening and closing her mouth like a goldfish. "I take that as a no." She turned back to glower at Lucas.

"Who are you?" Lydia stammered as she finally found her voice. Lucas and Kim glanced at each other, both wearing a pained expression, only Lucas' was deeper. "And what was that?" She added, nodding towards the fridge.

At this Kim smiled. "Magic." She gushed.

"Kim." Lucas warned but Kim shrugged before continuing.

"You got here last night, right?" Lydia nodded. "And in that time has anything unusual happened?"

Lydia wracked her brain trying to recall anything that was unusual but she drew blank as she slowly shook her head.

Kim pouted her lips in thought as she tapped her fingers against the side of the bottle as she became lost in her own thoughts. When that didn't help she stood up and began to look around.

Slowly Kim circled the kitchen as Lydia moved out of her way to stand against the kitchen counter and as Kim's eyes came back to land on Lydia she had an a-ha moment.

"There." She pointed next to Lydia who looked around and saw nothing out of the ordinary.

Lucas sat there watching with interest. His eyes zeroed in on what Kim had.

"The coffee machine." Kim announced.

"Huh?" Lydia looked from the coffee machine to Kim then back to the coffee machine.

"Your parents never owned a coffee machine. In fact, they don't even own a kettle." She stated, confusing Lydia even more. "You probably woke this morning and thought about having a cup of coffee." Kim went on to explain but it was all getting a bit too much for Lydia, who placed the full bottle of cider on the counter before holding her hands up.

"Stop." Lydia closed her eyes. She was convinced that she was in some weird dream.

Kim stilled. Her eyes blinking as they locked on to Lydia who began to massage her temples.

Lucas watched with a mixture of concern and interest. Concern that this was all a little too much for Lydia but interested to see how things would transpire. So far Lydia was handling things well but everyone had their limits.

Kim felt as though Lydia needed to know everything fast but there was such a thing as information overload. Lydia's memories had been wiped and even though they would come back Lucas felt the need for a gentler approach.

Standing up, Lucas moved until he was standing in front of Lydia. Gently and carefully, so as not to frighten her, he reached out to touch her arm.

"Lydia." his voice soft and calming. Lydia opened her eyes as she dropped her hands and looked into his eyes. She still struggled to understand how he'd been in her dreams when she'd had no recollection of him. "How about we start by explaining who we are to you and how we know your parents?" He asked gently as though trying to coax a frightened child.

Lydia nodded and allowed Lucas to lead her to the kitchen table.

Kim made a tutting sound before quickly joining them. She made a move to speak but a quick look from Lucas told her to be quiet.

"The three of us have been friends since childhood." Lucas began and Kim snorted only to be met by a warning glare from Lucas. "Our parents were friends too."

"Why don't I remember?" Lydia asked more to herself.

"This should be interesting." Kim snorted.

This time Lucas didn't even bother to look at Kim. He knew she was right.

Sucking in his lips he thought of the best way to phrase it.

"Something happened and you chose to leave. Your parents warned you that if you left you would never remember this place."

Wrong way to explain it as this gave Lydia more questions.

"What happened? Will I ever remember?"

This time Lucas looked at Kim for help but instead of offering she leaned back with a smirk on her face as she folded her arms. Kim was having far too much fun watching Lucas tiptoe around everything.

With a sigh Lucas looked back at Lydia. "Your memories will definitely return."

"When?" Lydia quickly responded.

Lucas shook his head. "I don't know. When the cottage decides."

"When the cottage decides." She repeated, half mocking and half disbelieving.

"Get to the good part." Kim goaded as she leaned forward, plastering on a huge smile.

Lucas shushed her but Lydia was intrigued.

"What good part?"

Lucas groaned as Lydia's eyes darted back and forth between them. When Lucas said nothing Kim lifted her hands and smacked them on the table.

"You two," she wiggled a finger back and forth from Lydia to Lucas, "are soul mates."

"Huh?" Lydia screwed up her face.

Lucas sighed but kept his eyes fixed to Lydia as he tried to gauge her reaction.

Mystic Valley series

"Your parents weren't normal parents either. They were a witch and warlock. And this cottage?" Kim continued. "This cottage was built over the entrance to the dark realms. Your parents protected it for a long time and now that they are gone it now becomes the responsibility of... can you guess? This is the real fun part." Kim smiled widely as both Lydia and Lucas sat there with their mouths open wide.

"Don't look at me like that." She scolded Lucas. "I was telling her what she needed to know. Now she might understand why her parents died."

No one said anything. Instead Lydia reached for Lucas' bottle and began drinking deeply. Only when she'd emptied it did she look at both Kim and Lucas.

"Now what happens?" She asked taking Lucas by surprise and making Kim clap with glee.

Chapter Four

With everything that had happened in the past 24 hours, Lydia felt drained. She didn't have it in her to challenge anything Kim had told her.

If Kim had said all this a week ago Lydia would have laughed. But she'd sat there in stunned silence taking it all in. She'd seen the fridge empty one minute then full the next. Then there was the matter of her memories. Lydia remembered nothing from her childhood.

The first memory she could recall was the day she started college. She remembered living in student accommodation and having no money or friends. She'd had no idea how she'd got there. She didn't know anything about herself apart from her name.

Lydia wanted answers. When she'd asked what happens next Lucas had been quick to jump in telling her that they'd discuss more tomorrow.

Something told Lydia that he was hiding something and she planned to find out what.

***

Lucas stood in the middle of the road, outside of the cottage, and pinched the bridge of his nose. For years he had imagined what it would be like to see Lydia again but all of them she had remembered him.

Being with her today had been hard. So many times he wanted to reach out and touch her. To feel her in his arms again and inhale her familiar scent. She had always smelled of freshly mowed grass mixed with a sea breeze. It was a smell that constantly lingered with him. All he ever needed to do was close his eyes and the aroma would engulf him.

Beside him Kim stood whistling as she looked around. She was desperate to talk to Lucas but she felt as though he needed few minutes.

Finally, Lucas dropped his hand and looked up at the sky.

"Does he know?" He sighed.

Kim paused from kicking the gravel she was kicking to try and feel Lucas' mood.

"Yup." She shrugged. Kim wasn't one to lie and she knew Lucas didn't want details.

Lucas nodded. "He's probably watching right now." He stated as he glanced at the trees.

"Probably." Kim joined Lucas and looked at the trees. There was no probably about it. She knew that Cole was sitting watching. "Lucas…" She started to say but her words trailed off as Lucas took to the sky, transforming into a beautiful hawk.

Lucas flew straight home. He loved to fly. Out of all the animals he could transform into a hawk was his favourite. There was something about the feel of the wind beneath his wings. There were no words to describe it. He felt free. His mind was always full of Lydia and flying was a chance to clear his thoughts. Subconsciously he knew that he always took flight in a hope to see her. That one day she would walk into Mystic Valley.

When Lucas entered his home his senses were met with the smell of freshly baked bread.

At twenty-four years old Lucas still lived at home with his parents. Many times he had thought about flying the coop and finding his own home but there were two things stopping him.

Firstly, it was the fact that he had things made for him here. His parents, Connor and Mary, who were also shapeshifters were a witch and warlock. His father was more of an indoors type person who loved to bake. His mother was the one who was always outside either collecting herbs from their herb garden or travelling to find rare ingredients.

Living with his parents meant he got a free ride, so to speak. He chipped in with **chores, but** they didn't ask him to pay his way because there was nothing to pay for.

Mystic Valley series

The second reason for him staying at home was because of Lydia. He never strayed too far in case she ever came back. Yesterday when she had finally returned he had felt her and instantly went searching for her in his dreams.

Growing up things between them had always been easy. They hung around in a group and life had been good. Lucas had always felt a strong connection to Lydia and he never understood why. Over time he had developed feelings for her but before he got a chance to make a move Cole had stolen a kiss.

It had broken Lucas' heart.

He was a teenage boy with hormones running wild. Cole had known Lucas had feelings for Lydia but that hadn't stopped him. Had Cole been attracted to Lydia? Of course, Lydia had always been beautiful. She was a pure soul with so much innocence.

Initially Lucas was convinced that Cole wasn't interested and merely saw Lydia as a means to one up Lucas but in the process it had set cracks in their friendship. Not only that, their group was sure that something was happening between Cole and Natalie. But after that day when Cole kissed Lydia, Natalie began to distance herself to the point where no one had seen her in two years. She still lived in the small cottage on the west point of Mystic Valley. The same cottage that Lydia had seen as she entered.

Natalie, the youngest of seven, had remained at home long after her siblings had departed.

Some say she spends her days mourning for the love that never was, something Lucas believed. Others say she allowed the dark spirits to enter her soul, but not one person has gone to check.

Lucas had hoped that when Lydia had left, Cole would have gone to Natalie but instead he became distant, angry and bitter.

You see, after that kiss with Lydia, Cole became almost spellbound. It seemed to happen overnight. He would follow Lydia around like a little lost puppy, which is ironic considering that's how he got her to kiss him.

Cole, a shapeshifter too, had never discovered his spirit animal so would often change from one animal to the next. He did have a fascination with baby animals joking that the girls loved them. So one day he had turned up at Lydia's home as an adorable, black, fluffy puppy and instantly Lydia picked him up to pet him, delivering a kiss. At this point Cole had transformed to his human form, taking Lydia by surprise. It was not how she had expected her first kiss to be.

After that Cole was relentless. He wore Lydia down and Lucas sat back and watched. Something he regretted because Lydia slowly began to develop feelings for Cole.

This didn't interfere with Lucas' friendship with Lydia. She was the same, giggly, sweet, teenage girl that he had fallen for and a huge part of him was convinced she had feelings for him too which was why he kissed her.

It was a week before her sixteenth birthday and they had been out by the river when Lydia slipped. Luckily for her, Lucas had been there and caught her before she fell in.

As their eyes locked something took over Lucas. When he had kissed her he had been overjoyed when she responded and when he reluctantly pulled away, brushing a loose strand of hair behind her ear he watched the happiness change to guilt.

She never said anything when Lucas had apologised as he walked her home but things had changed between them and he knew, just by catching her glimpses at him, that she felt something towards him.

On a couple of occasions Cole had noticed, sending Lucas warning glances.

Then came Lydia's sixteenth birthday. Her parents had thrown a small party. Everything was going well until Kim had suggested Lydia do the soul mate ritual. Something that can be done as soon as a person reaches their sixteenth birthday.

The colour drained had from Lydia's face.

At first Lucas had assumed that Kim's suggestion had been innocent, but as she glanced from Cole to Lucas he knew different. It wasn't until months later Lucas discovered that Kim had witnessed their first kiss.

Lydia's parents had thought it a great idea to perform the ritual which would tell them who their daughter's soul mate would be and future gatekeeper.

At the beginning, everyone assumed it would be Cole. Even Cole himself had made that assumption, but when the spirits had declared it to be Lucas all hell had broken loose.

The party had quickly ended. Everyone had been sent home and that was the last time her friends saw Lydia.

Her parents had been distraught, saying that Lydia could not handle the upset she had caused. On another occasion they said she didn't want the responsibility of being a gatekeeper so chose to leave. In the process removing all of her memories.

No one had any closure.

For the next several years' things dragged. Everyone had accepted that Lydia would never return. Everyone except Lucas. He believed deeply what the spirits said to be true. They were soul mates and they were meant to be together and when the time was right she would come back. She had. The problem was her memories hadn't. It felt as though Lucas was back at square one. Only this time he planned on fighting for Lydia.

Walking into the kitchen Lucas saw six freshly baked loaves of bread sitting on the table. As soon as his dad saw him he smiled. Without a word Connor cut a slice off one of the loaves, and after covering it with a thin layer of homemade butter, he handed it to Lucas. This was a regular occurrence for Lucas. He was often the chief taster in this house.

Taking a bite of the soft warm bread Lucas closed his eyes as he allowed the flavours to hit his taste buds.

"Garlic?" He finally managed to ask his eager looking dad who smiled widely.

"And coriander. What do you think?"

"You're on to a winner." He raised the bit of bread as you would a glass when you congratulate someone before stuffing the rest of it in his mouth.

More often than not Connor got a recipe spot on but there had been a few that had gone horribly wrong, such as the sweet cheese bread. For some unbeknownst reason he had thought it would be a great idea to combine sugar and cheese. To Lucas it had been disgusting.

Mystic Valley series

Without another word Connor turned back to his baking as Lucas climbed the stairs to his room. He was grateful for his parents in so many ways, but he loved the fact that they didn't pry. Yes, they would ask him how he was and they were always open for him to talk to but they felt that if Lucas had something on his mind then it was up to him to approach them instead of them forcing it out of him. It worked.

Lucas didn't want to talk about Lydia. What he did want to do was go to sleep and hopefully reach out to her through his dreams like the night before.

Chapter Five

Lydia was exhausted. After Lucas and Kim had left she had spent the rest of the evening unpacking. When she was finally done she was too tired to do anything other than climb into bed.

As she turned her bedroom light off Lydia felt as though her walls came to life. Even though she didn't witness it with her own eyes she was sure the fairies were moving.

Before today this would have unnerved Lydia but right now in the comfort of her bed she had the overwhelming feeling of calm. A calm that soon pulled her into sleep, where she quickly began dreaming.

She was in a field, sitting on a blanket with her eyes closed and her head tilted towards the sun allowing the vitamin D soak into her pores.

"You're really beautiful." A voice beside her said, causing Lydia's head to tilt towards it as her eyes fluttered open to see Lucas watching her intently.

With one hand Lucas reached to stroke her left cheek. Instinctively Lydia leaned into his hand, smiling as her eyes flirtatiously fluttered.

Lydia's heart picked up speed as Lucas leaned closer, pressing his forehead to hers.

"You're everything I ever wanted. All I'll ever need." He continued, his eyes burning with passion.

Lydia's eyes glanced towards his soft full lips making her suck in a breath as she pulled her bottom lip between her teeth. She wanted him to kiss her. She needed him to kiss her.

He looked as though he were about to. Lydia closed her eyes in preparation as she licked at her lips. But just as their lips almost touched Lydia heard the sound of a dog barking. Without thinking she moved her head away. It sounded like the dog was hurt.

Mystic Valley series

"Lydia stop." Lucas called out but Lydia didn't listen as she went in search for the dog. But it wasn't a dog. It was a cute little black puppy that melted Lydia's heart.

She was about to bend over to pick it up when she heard banging that grew in intensity.

Lydia looked around. Lucas was gone. The field was gone. Everywhere was dark and the puppy was now growling as the banging grew louder. So loud that it ripped her from her dreams. It was only then that she realised that the banging was coming from the front door.

Half asleep and confused by who could be knocking at this time of night Lydia slowly crept out of her room and down the stairs.

Lydia's heart hammered in her chest as the banging continued. She felt sick with fear.

"Who's there?" Her voice trembled and instantly the banging stopped.

"It's Lucas." A voice quickly answered causing her fear to quickly disperse as she opened the door to see him standing there taking deep breaths.

"Lucas?" Her voice confused. "What's wrong?"

Without answering Lucas took two long strides, closing the distance between them before taking her face in his hands and kissing her hard.

At first Lydia was taken by surprise. Surprise soon gave way to passion. Passion she had never felt before.

Their hands began to explore. Their clothes nothing more than a heap on the floor.

The door was still left open, casting moonlight into the cottage, as Lucas lifted Lydia before pushing himself inside her. They both cried out. Lucas pressed her against the wall, penetrating her deep and hard as he covered her mouth with his own.

As their passion escalated, sparks erupted from the floor. Neither of them noticing, too lost in their pleasure.

The sparks turned to fire as Lydia tasted her orgasm. Lucas pushed deeper and faster. His mouth moving to her neck. He sucked, licked and bit just as he began to climax. They both moaned and held onto each other.

Their hearts hammered in their chests as they tried to steady their breathing.

Lucas slowly kissed his way back up to Lydia's mouth, this time gentler.

They didn't need words. Something had changed. Even though their bodies were still as one they were still held together by an invisible thread.

"Lydia, I feel..."

"I feel it too."

Words couldn't describe it. It was something so deep. So revitalising. Lydia may not have her memories back, yet, but she felt more connected to Lucas than anyone. It wasn't just physically. It wasn't just her heart either. She could feel everything Lucas felt. She could hear his thoughts and she knew that he was experiencing the exact same thing.

They should have been scared, instead, they both felt peace, contentment and love.

Without lowering her, Lucas closed and locked the front door. Leaving their clothes on the floor he carried Lydia upstairs. Neither of them realising what had happened around them as they made love.

The cottage was back to normal only igniting again when they climbed into bed and their need grew.

As the flames of the cottage danced to Lucas and Lydia's passion, a crow that was perched in the trees squawked loudly and angrily before flying away.

Mystic Valley series

***

Lydia woke feeling giddy. As her eyes fluttered open she saw Lucas sleeping next to her. He lay on his back with an arm behind his head. His eyes closed and a small smile curved at his lips.

Her eyes roamed his body. He was completely naked with only a blanket protecting his modesty. As her eyes studied each contour she recalled everything that had happened last night. Lydia had never felt so alive. She hadn't realised that sex could be so explosive. She only had Steve to compare to but right now Steve was the furthest from her mind.

She had met Lucas yesterday and immediately felt drawn to him. She dreamed about him. Her whole body had yearned for him. When he arrived at her house last night she knew she needed him. They needed each other.

No words were spoken out loud. They communicated with their minds and bodies. The two were completely in sync with the other, knowing exactly how to stimulate pleasures that had never been touched before. In those hours Lydia had felt more complete than she had ever felt before.

As Lydia's eyes worked their way back up Lucas' body they fell on the odd shaped pendant around his neck. It was unusual and she wasn't sure what it was meant to be. There was something familiar about it and when she reached out to touch it she was surprised to discover that it felt warm.

Turning towards her bedside table, Lydia reached for the small box. Opening it she retrieved her own unusual pendant and gasped when she felt the heat it expelled.

With urgency Lydia quickly moved back to Lucas and moved her pendant towards his.

As soon as they touched Lydia gasped louder this time as Lucas' eyes flew open.

The two pendants melded together, creating some type of spike.

On impulse, Lucas moved his hand to the pendants and ran his fingers along it. His eyes growing wide in confusion as he felt various etchings.

Looking at Lydia he saw the same confusion in her eyes.

"I…" Her voice trailed off. She was at a loss for words. What did this mean? Was this something to do with being soul mates? Did this confirm that they were?

Lucas had read her thoughts. His own questions mirroring Lydia's. He had never known what it was but he had known it was special. Lydia's parents had given it to him on the day she had left. They never explained what it meant just that it was connected to Lydia.

"Lydia?" He whispered, reaching for her and pulling her down to his mouth.

Lydia moved quickly, discarding the blanket and climbing on top, allowing him to enter her.

This time, in the morning light, they watched not only each other but witnessed the cottage come alive. Sparks flying before setting the entire room a light.

Neither of them feared the fire. It only ignited their passion more.

As they both began to climax they impulsively reached for the spike. It burned and pulsed as their hands clasped around it.

Their moans escalated. The fire raged on, only subsiding as Lydia collapsed on top of Lucas. Both gasping for breath, they each looked at their hands that had been holding the spike. In the palm of each hand lay freshly etched swirls.

"Bonded." They both whispered as they clasped their hands together, feeling it deep inside. Their new scars were pulsating.

Their chests heaved as Lydia lay on top Lucas, both blissfully happy in their closeness. For at least ten minutes anyway.

"I need to get my memories back." Lydia suddenly told Lucas as she lifted her head to look at him. He nodded in agreement as he brushed his knuckles against her cheek.

It was something he wanted badly, but he feared how she would react. He didn't want to lose her again.

Reading his thoughts Lydia gave Lucas' hand a gentle squeeze. "I only turned up here yesterday and so many things have happened in such a short space of time. Things that last week my mind wouldn't have been able to comprehend. Then there is this," she lifted their hands, "and us. I don't understand it but I know it feels right."

Lucas watched her intently, listening and feeling all of her emotions as she spoke. Lydia was everything he had always wanted. He knew that he would give her anything she ever wanted and do everything in his powers and beyond to protect her.

"I want to know everything."

With a sigh Lucas nodded before taking a deep breath and telling Lydia everything from as far back as he could remember. He didn't leave anything out. He watched her face as he retold the story of her relationship with Cole.

When he had finally finished they both lay side by side, on the bed. The blanket was back on top of them and Lucas trailed his fingers along Lydia's arm as he waited with bated breath to see how she would react.

He felt her before she even spoke and he was relieved to know she was calm.

"So that was really you in my dreams?" Lucas nodded. "You knew everything I dreamt and you were part of it?" He nodded again. "And the puppy was Cole?" She asked, referring to the puppy in her dreams.

Lucas nodded once more. "He had somehow managed to penetrate your dreams too."

"Hoping to kiss me before you?"

"I think so." Lucas nodded.

"And that's why you appeared last night?"

Lucas smiled widely. When Cole had appeared in their dreams Lucas had woken himself up and flew straight here. He couldn't allow Cole to kiss her. He promised himself to fight for her.

"I thought I was still dreaming." Colour crept into Lydia's face as she recalled how passionate Lucas was and how they had made love right there with the door wide open.

"If it is a dream I don't want it to end." Lucas whispered causing Lydia to blush deeper as she rolled onto her front, covering most of her face with her pillow as she peeked at Lucas. She was still struggling to grasp that she had had sex with a stranger within twenty-four hours of meeting him. Not only that, she felt he was the sexiest piece of eye candy she had ever seen who knew exactly what buttons to press.

"The feelings mutual." Lucas chuckled, reading her thoughts.

Lydia buried her head in the pillow and groaned loudly. She had forgotten that they could now read each other's thoughts.

"I think it's the bond." Lucas lifted his right hand to see if the swirls were still there and they were. With his left hand he ran his fingers along them.

"I'm married." Lydia suddenly whispered, pulling a black cloud over the mood.

"I know." Lucas dropped his hand to look at Lydia.

"Doesn't it bother you?" Lydia sat up to look at him.

Lucas shrugged. "A little bit. But the way I see it, all that happened because you lost your memories."

"I still don't have my memories."

"But you're here." Lucas pointed out with a smile making a small smile appear on Lydia's face, which only grew with intensity.

"You're right." She nodded. "And as soon as my memories are back I am going to divorce that bastard." She said with determination as she jumped out of bed.

Lucas chuckled as he watched Lydia moved to get dressed.

Mystic Valley series

"In the meantime I really need a large mug of coffee."

Chapter Six

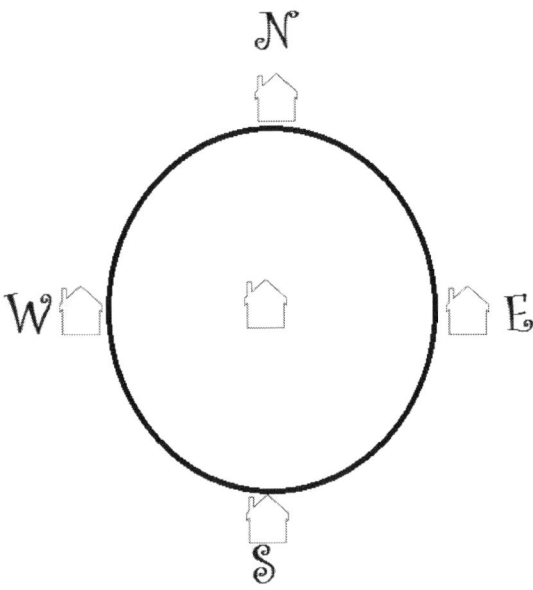

Whilst Lydia made coffee, Lucas drew a simple diagram with the cottage in the centre. The cottage was situated over the entrance to the dark realms. On the outer edges of Mystic Valley were four cottages, each situated on a different cardinal compass point. Each of these housed the guardians, those who not only stopped normal humans from wandering into Mystic Valley but also as an added precaution in case the gatekeepers couldn't control the entrance to the dark realm and the seal broke.

As Lydia sipped her coffee she watched intently as Lucas explained who lived where – Lucas and his family lived in the northern cottage, Kim and her family in the east, Cole and his family in the south, and Natalie and her family in the west.

Natalie wasn't a name she had recalled hearing about but she thought she would leave that for another time.

"Question." Lydia placed her cup down as she looked from the map to Lucas, who was hunched over it. "With us being…" her voice trailed off as she tried to figure out the right words. Bonded? Soulmates?

"Soulmates." Lucas glanced up with a wide smile.

Lydia nodded. "Soulmates." She could happily say that. "And I am supposed to be a gatekeeper. Does that make you one too?"

Lucas paused thoughtfully. "I suppose it does."

Which is exactly what Lydia thought. The next question would have normally felt completely alien, but these weren't normal circumstances.

"Does that mean that you should be living here… with me?"

It wasn't an invite, per se. It was a thought. A thought that made sense. Briefly, it made her laugh and shake her head. Had she lost her mind? Talk about a roller coaster. Within twenty-four hours of meeting Lucas they had bonded in almost every way possible and now she was asking him to move in.

Lucas put down the pen he was holding to turn to look at Lydia, a goofy expression on his face as he watched the look on her face.

"Are you asking me to move in with you? Already?" He mock gasped, putting his hands to his cheeks. "My parents warned me about girls like you taking advantage of sweet innocent young boys like me."

This made Lydia throw her head back and laugh. There was definitely nothing innocent about the things Lucas did to her and how he made her feel.

Lucas grabbed her, pulling her close and leaving lingering kisses along her neck and up to her jawline.

"Do you think you could handle me being here 24/7?" The words rumbled in his throat, sending shivers throughout Lydia's body.

"No." She was quick to add. "I may combust." She told him seriously, her eyes closed, enjoying the feel of his lips on her skin.

It was Lucas' turn to laugh just as someone knocked at the door.

"Ignore it." Lucas growled.

"I can hear you both in there." Kim's voice shouted and without waiting she opened the front door making Lydia gasped.

"I thought the door was locked."

"It was." Lucas answered.

"Spare key." Kim smiled widely as she took in the scene before her. "My, my, don't you two look cosy." She beamed as she walked past them both, going straight for the fridge. This time she pulled out a can of coke out. As she opened it Kim turned to lean against the counter whilst sizing up the situation before her. "You two had sex last night. Lots of it." She stated before taking a long swig of the coke.

Lydia was about to deny it, feeling embarrassed, but Kim waved a hand in front of her.

"The cottage made a huge announcement about it. We could feel the heat from our house." She teased but something told Lydia that Kim was being serious.

Gasping, Lydia looked at Lucas. The same thoughts running through his mind.

The sparks and the fire… they were real. Lydia had thought she had imagined it. How was that even possible?

Kim said nothing. She just stood there wearing smug smile as she took careful sips of her coke as she watched Lydia's reaction.

"How do you have a spare key?" Lucas asked, wanting to change the subject.

Kim shook her head, rolled her eyes and pulled out a seat at the kitchen table. "Each house has one."

This was true. It was something Lucas had forgotten because no one had ever had to use it.

"My father demanded that I come over and check that you hadn't burned to death." Kim said as more of an afterthought as she leaned over to look at what Lucas had been drawing. "Neat." She nodded before turning to look at Lydia. "How are the memories? Did the crazy sex break the dam?" She asked in seriousness.

Lydia blinked, then blinked again. She wondered if Kim was always like this, if she was then it was going to get annoying fast.

"Not yet." Lucas huffed, more at the fact that Kim was so flippant about the sex.

"Well you need to up your game then. Maybe try a few new positions. Push deeper-"

"Enough." Lydia put her fingers to her temples. The moment Kim had stepped through that front door she had felt a twinge of a migraine and the more Kim spoke the worse it became.

Kim was about to make a smart retort but she noticed Lydia's hand and moved to grab her wrist. As soon as she touched Lydia, Lucas placed a hand on top of Kim's. Kim reacted quickly though as she moved her other hand to flip Lucas' hand over.

"Woah." Kim's eyes grew wide as she looked at the scars on the palms of their hands. Before she could examine them closer both Lucas and Lydia snatched their hands away. "You guys really are soulmates." She said in disbelief.

This took Lucas by surprise as for the first time it sounded like Kim hadn't believed it until now.

Something crossed Kim's face and Lucas wasn't sure what as Kim was always good at hiding her feelings but there was definitely something there. Within seconds it was gone and Kim was jumping up and heading towards the front door.

"I'll let my parents know that you are fine and that you and Lucas were just having lots of earth shattering sex." She lifted a hand in the air as though waving. Lydia almost choked on the air she was breathing and as Lucas patted her back, Kim stopped at the front room. "And if you want your memories back…" She thoughtfully drummed her fingers on the open front door. "You may want to try your parents' bedroom." Then she left, slamming the door behind her.

As soon as Kim had left Lucas turned back to Lydia, who sat there thoughtfully. She had arrived here two nights ago and in that time she had been too scared to even enter her parents' bedroom.

"You'll get used to her." Lucas said, referring to Kim. "Believe it or not, the two of you were really close."

Lydia made a scoffing sound but quickly stopped. She couldn't say it wasn't true as she didn't remember her previous life. She did, however, think that she must have had a screw lose if she constantly put up with Kim's crap.

"Am I a shapeshifter too?" Lydia had no idea where this thought came from. Well she did, but why now? Deep down she knew she was trying to change the subject so as to avoid going to her parents' bedroom.

"You were. I don't see why it would be any different now."

Lydia knew why it could be different. For the last eight years Lydia had lived as a normal human. She had no memories of this life here and she had a feeling that when the block was put on her mind, one was also put on her shape shifting abilities because she certainly hadn't shifted in the past eight years.

As Lydia sat there trying to avoid the inevitable, Lucas stood and held out his right hand. Lydia looked at it and the fresh swirl of scars before lifting her left hand, which mirrored Lucas' right, and placed it in his.

It was time to get this over and done with.

Mystic Valley series

Chapter Seven

This was the one room that Lydia felt apprehensive about entering. What if she opened the door and was instantly hit by a flood of memories and emotions that rocked her to the core? So many that she broke down and cried. But on the other hand, she worried that she would open that door and feel nothing. No memories. No emotions. Nothing. This was her biggest fear and it made her feel nauseous, especially because it was a realisation that maybe her memories wouldn't come back. Her childhood would be this huge, black, cavernous hole. She wouldn't remember her parent's laughter, their hugs, their kisses or them telling her that she would be okay. It wasn't as if she could make new memories with them. They were gone.

"How did my parents die?" She asked Lucas as they ascended the narrow staircase. "I mean really die." It wasn't until being here that she sensed the whole story of a car accident was just a fabrication.

"Your parents didn't drive." Lucas informed her as they reached the top of the stairs, bringing Lydia to a stop as she looked at the back of Lucas as he moved to her parents' bedroom door.

"What do you mean, they didn't drive?"

As Lucas reached for the handle he paused and looked back at Lydia, realising she wasn't following.

"That solicitor told me they were killed in a car accident." She exclaimed.

Lucas sucked in his lips. He'd knew this conversation was inevitable but he also hoped it wouldn't come.

Lydia's head was reeling. She had been told one thing and now another. She didn't know what was true and what wasn't. So many things were happening and her mind was in a spin.

Lucas walked back and reached for her. "There was an accident but we had to tell you one that you would believe." He paused as he tried to think of the correct words. "If last week someone had come to you and said magic was real, would you have believed them?"

Lydia blinked, then blinked again before finally shaking her head.

"Exactly." He brushed his knuckles along her face. "There was an incident where the entrance to the dark realm was opened. A few beings escaped. Your parents tried to defend themselves but were unprepared." His voice trailed off, hoping she would understand the extent of his words.

"Where?" Lydia whispered, a sense of grief for the loss of parents she didn't know filled her.

Lucas sighed. He knew Lydia wanted answers but he wasn't sure she was ready. "Can we not talk about this later? I promise to tell you everything you need to know after we've looked around your parent's room." He gave a pensive expression, mirroring Lydia's.

"You're stalling." She rebutted.

"So are you." Lucas was quick to respond, knowing full well that Lydia was scared to go into her parent's bedroom. He didn't need to be bonded to figure that out.

For a few moments they stood there face to face, Lydia wearing a stoic expression as she readied herself to argue. To demand he tell her about her parents. But she knew it would be fruitless. She could try to read his mind but it seemed to happen in short, sporadic bursts. Sometimes there were images, both clear and blurry. Other times she heard his voice. It was strange. Almost like having your ears fully submerged in water whilst trying to listen to someone talking.

"Fine." Lydia blew out a big breath. "But I want to know everything."

Lucas gave a slow nod before turning to walk back to the bedroom door. Taking a deep breath, he turned the handle as he exhaled.

As the door opened a cloud of darkness seeped out.

Without waiting to see if Lydia was following, Lucas stepped into the room and became immersed in blackness and he blindly searched for the curtains.

At first Lucas struggled to open the heavy, red velvet, curtains, but after a few tugs they eventually relented but only letting in a small amount out of light causing Lucas to frown. The curtains were wide open. The sun outside was high but instead of seeping through the windows it merely stopped.

Confusion turned to ignorance as he shrugged and turned to look at the room. It wasn't until then that he noticed that everything in the room was dark. Not just because of the little light penetrating through the window pane but every piece of furniture, ornament, bedding... everything, was a mixture of blacks and greys. It was as though all colour had drained from everything.

The wooden handcrafted furniture was black, when Lucas knew this wasn't even possible. Not unless Lydia's parents had chosen to paint the furniture, but as Lucas stepped forward for a closer inspection he noticed that there was no paint.

"What is this?" Lydia's voice whispered from the doorway.

For a brief moment Lucas had forgotten she was even there and looked up, the confusion evident in his face but as he took in Lydia his confusion only grew.

The further Lydia stepped into the room the more the colour drained from her until she was standing there in a mixture of greys and blacks.

Lydia gasped, but her eyes were on Lucas.

Lifting his hand, Lucas flipped it back and forth noticing his own hand was grey.

Without a word he moved towards the door and stuck his arm out. Immediately the colour returned.

For the next few minutes Lucas continued to put his arm in and out of the room until Lydia spoke.

"What is this?"

"I…I don't know." He stammered, moving to step back into the room. Immediately he started to move around the room, trying to open the drawers and cupboards, all seemed locked but without a keyhole to open them.

Whilst Lucas inspected the room, Lydia moved towards the bed where boxes lay on top. Being gentle she lifted the flaps of the boxes to peer inside.

"Christmas decorations." Lydia muttered to herself. She had forgotten that it was late November and Christmas was just around the corner.

Lucas turned to look noticing they too lacked colour.

"I think the cottage is in mourning." He stated, more to himself.

Lydia nodded but said nothing as they both stood there wondering what to do next. As her eyes roamed the room she saw pictures of herself on each bedside table. The sight of them being there pulled at her heart. It was something so small but it made her feel loved. It made her want to know her parents. No… she needed to remember them,

As soon as the thought entered her mind something in the room clicked. Instantly, Lydia and Lucas turned their heads to a set of drawers to see that the top one was now open.

Lucas glanced at Lydia, who remained riveted to the spot, before moving to look inside the drawer.

All he found was an envelope with Lydia's name written on the front.

Turning, he held out the envelope. When Lydia didn't move he walked towards her.

"I can't." She shook her head, feeling overwhelmed with fear and sadness at what the letter may say.

When she refused to take it from him Lucas sighed before opening it himself.

Slowly he pulled out a single piece of folded paper whilst gauging Lydia's reaction.

She nodded for him to continue.

Chapter Eight

"How far away is your parent's house?" Lydia asked as they stepped outside. The cool, crisp, air nipped at her nose and cheeks, making her pull the collar of her coat closer.

"About ten miles." Lucas shrugged before making a move to the road.

"Ten miles?" She gasped, following Lucas whilst looking around. "Shouldn't we take the car?" She pointed back to it whilst trying to catch up to Lucas who stopped at the entrance of the cottage's driveway.

"Nope." He smiled whilst shaking his head. His eyes twinkled as Lydia pouted over walking so far. She had been so used to living in London and either driving everywhere or using another type of transport. Walking more than one hundred metres was not something she ever did.

With a shimmer Lucas transformed into a magnificent, brown, horse. If Lydia had blinked she would have missed the transformation.

As the horse neighed and nodded its head Lydia stood there with her mouth opened wide, unable to comprehend what had just happened.

You'll catch flies if you leave your mouth open like that.

The sound of Lucas' voice spoke inside her head.

Instantly Lydia closed her mouth, but never once taking her eyes off the horse, whilst keeping a safe distance.

Are you going to get on or not?

Lucas teased, inside her head.

"Lucas? Is that you?" Lydia stammered as she craned her neck to look in the horses deep brown eyes.

The horse neighed and nodded as it turned around to look her in the eyes.

Get on.

"How?"

There was no saddle or anything to help her get up on top of the horse.

Without a word the horse sat down and waited patiently as Lydia nervously stared at the horse before taking tentative steps closer.

Before climbing on top she ran her hands across the horse's neck and instantly felt an overwhelming calmness.

***

A few minutes before they arrived at Lucas' family home the horse stopped and lowered itself so Lydia could slide off. Taking a few steps back Lydia watched as Lucas transformed back into his human form. It was strange but also cool at the same especially because the end result was Lucas standing there completely naked. A part of her did not want to hand over his clothes.

"Easy tiger." Lucas chuckled. "There are eyes and ears everywhere." He said in response to the visions he saw in Lydia's mind which were crystal clear and in great detail.

Lydia blushed before chuckling herself.

"All in good time." Lucas winked as he hurried to get dressed before taking Lydia's hand.

From where they stood Lydia could make out the outline of a house, almost twice the size of the cottage. As they neared she could see a woman standing outside using her hand to shield the sun out of her eyes as she looked in their direction. Instantly Lydia knew it to be Lucas' mum.

She stood at average height, wearing dark coloured trousers, black boots, and a big, thick, multi-coloured jumper. Her hair was a dirty blonde colour that looked thick and bushy and almost to her waist. She had somehow managed to tie half of it off her face but as the wind blew it picked up the rest which acted like long arms wrapping themselves tightly around her.

Her face was weather-beaten, from spending the majority of the days outside in the garden, but even so Lydia could tell that she was very beautiful, with twinkling blue eyes that mirrored her sons.

"Lydia." The words were like a sigh as they left his mothers lips as a smile spread across her face.

At first Lydia blinked wondering how she knew her name, but then she remembered…

"Hi." Lydia smiled nervously.

Before losing her memories she may have been close to this woman but right now she was a stranger and it felt as though she were meeting her boyfriend's parents for the first time.

"Look at you." She gushed, before taking Lydia off guard and pulling her into her arms and squeezing tightly.

Lydia's body went rigid as she nervously laughed.

"Mum, she doesn't remember you." Lucas interjected.

Lucas' mum pulled away but kept both hands on Lydia as she looked to her son and then back to Lydia. "Still spellbound?" She frowned, acting as though Lydia had lost her hearing.

Both Lydia and Lucas nodded.

She made a few hmmm noises as she glanced between her son and Lydia as she tried to think about the situation.

"I didn't think our spell was that strong."

"Your spell?" Lydia and Lucas chorused but his mum shrugged it away, releasing one of Lydia's arms whilst moving the other to take Lydia's hand.

"Oh." She said in surprise before lifting Lydia's hand for a closer inspection. "You bonded." She smiled, looking towards her son.

Lydia blushed. It felt as though the mark on her hand was a mark that announced to the world that they had had sex. She remembered living in London when seeing a clear sign of humans getting it on was a disgusting bruise on their necks, which they called love bites or hickeys. At least this was prettier, even if it did seem to be permanent.

Within seconds his mum frowned again. "I would have thought the bonding unlocked the spell." She muttered to herself as she steered Lydia into the house. "Normally when the two halves of a soul find their way back to each other all the spells break away." She told them both before fixing Lydia with a serious stare. "You did climax, didn't you? My son was sufficient in the-"

"Mum." Lucas blanched feeling mortified as Lydia went a deep shade of red but his mum wasn't deterred.

"I need to know. If you didn't satisfy her then that may be the reason the spell is still intact." She tried to reason.

Lucas was about to mumble something about their sex life being of no concern of anyone but the two of them when Lydia spoke. Her embarrassment now left. In its place was amusement.

"Lucas was more than satisfactory. Apparently we lit up the entire cottage." Lydia gave a side glance to Lucas who returned with a smug expression.

His mum sighed then released Lydia's hand to pat her son. "Good job." She congratulated him.

A short, loud, laugh escaped Lydia as her hand quickly moved to her mouth. She was going to remember this conversation for a very long time and bring it up with Lucas at every given opportunity.

Just then a man, a little under six foot with a protruding stomach stepped into the room. "I thought I heard voices." He smiled widely showing crooked, white, teeth. He looked like an older, shorter and rounder version of Lucas.

He was wearing a loose pair of jeans with a white t-shirt and an apron. Not that the apron seemed to be protecting him from anything as he was practically covered from head to toe in flour.

"Well I never." His eyes twinkled when he saw Lydia.

"She doesn't remember us." His wife quickly answered.

"Still?"

"Strong as ever." His wife quickly answered before looking back to Lydia. "That is Connor, Lucas' father." She pointed out.

"Pleased to meet you." Lydia smiled.

"Oh how silly of me." Lucas' mum quickly spoke again. "I didn't tell you my name." She smacked her forehead with the heel of her hand. "My name is Mary and I'm-"

"Lucas' mum." Lydia smiled and Mary nodded.

"Come have some freshly baked muffins. I just made some oats and syrup ones which are still nice and hot." Connor beckoned. "They always taste better when not long out of the oven." He winked as Lydia, Lucas and Mary followed.

"Oh wow." Lydia's eyes grew wide as she stepped into the large kitchen to see almost every surface covered in either flour or freshly baked food. "Do you sell them?" She asked, intrigued, as she accepted a freshly baked muffin.

Connor laughed and patted his stomach. "Does this tummy look as though I sell them?" He teased, rubbing it.

Lydia said nothing, fear of sounding rude, as she tore off a piece of the muffin. Instantly steam rose from it and releasing an amazing aroma.

"We swap things with the other families." Lucas added. "The Willoughby's have medicine, the Everly's have cattle, and the Shapley's do carpentry." He finished off with a mouthful of food.

"What family is Kim from?" Lydia asked as she sat down at the kitchen table. "This is really good." She looked to Connor. "Best cake I have ever had."

Connor gave a large toothy grin.

"Oh, you've met Kim?" Mary asked as she attempted to make some space on one of the counters before giving up.

Lydia nodded. "The day after I arrived her and Lucas turned up at my house."

"Kim's an Everly." Lucas informed Lydia, leaning back against one of the kitchen counters as he started to eat his second muffin.

"And what are your surnames?" Lydia realised that she didn't know much about Lucas. But she could remember every single contour of his body and exactly how to please him.

I heard that. Lucas spoke inside her head.

In her mind she pulled a tongue and Lucas laughed.

Lydia had to admit that this telepathy had its uses. They could have their own private conversation without anyone hearing.

"Are you meaning to tell me that you have been courting this lovely lady without telling her your name?" Connor teased and shook his head.

"Dad, no one says courting any more." Lucas rolled his eyes. "Plus," he reached for a third muffin, "I've known Lydia my entire life. It slipped my mind to mention it." He shrugged, not seeing the big deal.

"Newbury. Our surname is Newbury." Mary spoke close to Lydia. "And in case you hadn't noticed, the first letter in all of our surname pinpoints to where we are on a compass."

Lydia paused, mid bite. She hadn't actually thought about it but now she saw it, it made sense but in an odd way. But it also got her thinking… "Before I got married my surname was Smith."

"No dear." Mary shook her head. "It's Cafferty."

"Cafferty?" Lydia asked in confusion as she looked around the room. Everyone nodded. "Then why Smith?" She didn't understand. It is one thing to take her memories but why her surname. It was just a name.

"Smith is a very common surname. Easy to blend in." Mary pointed out.

"Plus," Lucas looked to his parents before looking at Lydia. "All supernatural being's surnames end in Y."

Lydia pulled a face. "Really?"

"Really?" The three of them chorused.

"So if you kept your surname it would have been easy for others to have tracked you down." Mary stated.

Lydia hmmmed. It was confusing but not something she planned on dwelling on right now. She wanted to remember.

"Soooo." She drawled. "How do I get my memories back?"

Chapter Nine

For the next few hours, Lydia listened intently to Mary and Connor, as they talked about the day the memory spell was put on her.

Lydia had been the one to beg for the spell. Her parents had tried to talk her out of it but she had been adamant, assuring them that this is what she needed and if she was meant to be in Mystic Valley then she would find her way back.

On the night of her sixteenth birthday, after everyone else had left the party, the elders remained and performed a ritual. None of them had performed a memory spell to this extent before. Normally they had performed simple memory charms that lasted less than twenty-four hours. This was something different.

At the end of the ceremony Lydia was to drink from a chalice, filled with a sleeping drug. As soon as it took effect Mr Langford, the solicitor, drove Lydia away. With his help she was given a fake surname and family history along with a place to live in student accommodations. The rest they were unsure of so Lydia explained what she had been doing since then.

From time to time Mr Langford would drop by letting Lydia's parents know how she was getting on.

"How's the cottage doing?" Mary finally asked, taking both Lydia and Lucas off guard.

"The cottage?" Lydia shook her head in confusion, glancing at Lucas for some clarification but he shrugged.

"Anything different about it? Is it acting in unusual ways?" Mary pressed.

Lydia could have answered that it was unusual for any home to act in any way, apart from standing as a solid structure. Was it odd that it produced a coffee machine or that drinks appeared in the fridge? Absolutely, but Lydia didn't think that was what she meant. Especially when Lucas and Kim had informed her that the cottage was magical.

"Jim and Angelica's bedroom is grey." Lucas spoke and it was the first time Lydia had heard him say her parents' names. Lydia herself had only discovered their names in the documents. She was ashamed to admit that she hadn't looked through the paperwork. She knew she should because there may be something in there that would explain how to get her memories back but she couldn't bring herself to open it. Maybe if she had she would have known her real surname.

"Sounds like she is in mourning." Connor solemnly interjected.

"She?" Lydia continued to act confused.

Connor shrugged. "I like to think of the cottage as a she."

"Is this house... alive?" The word felt foreign in that context.

Connor shook his head. "The cottage is the only one due to the fact that it is in the very core of Mystic Valley and its epicentre is the entrance to the dark realm."

"Anyway," Mary interrupted, "Cafferty's have been in that cottage going back hundreds upon hundreds of years. According to legend, every time the owners die the cottage mourns for the loss until the rightful heir takes over."

"Rightful heir?" Lydia echoed, not liking the sound of that.

Mary nodded.

"But what if I don't want to live in the cottage? What if I don't want to stay in Mystic Valley?"

Mary opened and closed her mouth like a goldfish as she looked at her family for help.

Lucas' stare penetrated Lydia's. He never voiced anything outwardly or inwardly but Lydia knew what was going on in his mind. She could feel the worry and dread.

"I'm not saying that I don't want to." She quickly added. "But this is all new to me. I don't remember everything or everyone. To me you are all strangers who I have just met."

And there it was. Lucas felt as though he had been slapped in the face. Instantly Lydia felt bad.

"You'll feel differently as soon as you get your memories back." Mary was quick to reassure, when she felt the change in atmosphere.

"If." Lydia was quick to correct but Mary shook her head as she reached to take Lydia's hand.

"When." Mary spoke with finality.

Lydia hoped that she was right. The last couple of days had been intense but as she looked to Lucas, who never took his eyes from her, she knew she wanted to be with him. That feeling alone scared her. Even when she had suggested that they live together she hadn't felt afraid, but the idea of her memories coming back and ruining everything scared her. What if they came back and she hated Lucas?

***

Mary had suggested that they do the spell again, only this time in reverse. The problem they had was not all those who participated in the spell were alive or able to do the spell.

Both of Natalie's parents were sick. Ironic when they were the ones who dealt in medicine. Her mother suffers from Alzheimer's and her father suffers from muscular sclerosis. Out of all her siblings Natalie was the only one who chose to stay at home and care for parents, thus resulting in her taking on all the responsibilities her parents shared.

She was a fast learner. Mary and Connor had praised Natalie a lot.

According to Lucas though, Natalie did not like Lydia, so Lydia was unsure how this whole spell undoing would play out.

Time would tell.

Then there was Cole. Lucas had argued that one of his parents could do the spell but his father was adamant that all the casters had to be on the same level.

Whereas Lydia was nervous at the prospect of meeting more new faces that knew her, Lucas felt as though he were going to get an ulcer. He didn't mind talking to Natalie. As far as he saw it she would be easy to convince, but Cole… Cole was a different matter entirely and if he had his choice he wouldn't have Cole anywhere near Lydia.

Lucas and Lydia had decided to walk home. Neither said much. They were happy to walk side by side, hand in hand, enjoying their time together whilst they both worried about the prospect of Lydia getting her memories back.

Lydia's thoughts were the usual, mainly circling around the fact that what if she got her memories back and didn't like what she remembered.

Lucas' thoughts were mainly focused around Cole. Lydia had always been a kind hearted soul and he worried that getting her memories back she would take pity on Cole, who, in turn, would use this to his advantage and worm his way back in.

Not that he doubted Lydia's feelings for him. He just worried that the memories would alter them.

"Where have you guys been?"

The pair of them had just stepped into the cottage's garden and saw Kim sitting on the front step with the front door wide open drinking a can of coke.

"How the heck did you get into the house?" Lydia asked in alarm as Kim stood up and shrugged.

"The cottage likes me."

Lydia looked at Lucas in panic. She didn't like the idea of anyone being able to just waltz into the cottage whilst no one was home just because the cottage apparently liked them.

"Manners Kim." Lucas rolled his eyes but didn't act surprised. He was convinced that Kim came built without manners or fear.

Kim pulled a face. "I could say the same thing when I just asked where the two of you have been and neither answered."

"Not that it is of any of your concern…" Lucas walked past Kim and into the cottage, pulling Lydia behind him. "But we went to see my parents."

"Oh how cute. Getting all cosy with the family." Sarcasm dripped from her mouth as she followed them inside and almost running into the back of Lydia.

As soon as Lucas had stepped into the cottage he looked up to see the upstairs of the cottage lacking colour. It was like some type of mist that was creeping to the stairs and slowly moving and destroying all the colour.

"We left the bedroom door open." Lucas hurried to say, before rushing upstairs.

"What is that?" Kim hadn't noticed it the first time she had arrived but there was no way she could miss it now.

"The cottage is in mourning." Lydia whispered as she watched the colour from the top two steps drain away, turning them a dark grey.

"Hopefully that stops it." Lucas reappeared at the top of the stairs.

"Oh cool." Kim looked at Lucas. The swirls or blacks, whites and greys only made him look more attractive. "It is amazing how good things look in black and white." She said in appreciation, causing Lydia look at her in disbelief. "What?" Kim shrugged and gave an innocent smile.

Rolling her eyes Lydia walked into the kitchen and began to make herself a coffee.

"What's the goss'?" Kim asked as her and Lucas followed Lydia into the kitchen.

Lucas moved to the kitchen table whilst Kim moved to grab another can of coke from the fridge before, leaning against the counter and tapping the lid.

"My parents think that we should do a spell circle." Lucas told Kim but his eyes were on Lydia, watching her every move.

Kim raised an eyebrow more for what Lucas had said but she followed his line of sight. She watched Lydia who was completely unaware of the effect she had on Lucas.

"How do you feel about all of this?" Kim asked Lydia. It took a few moments before Lydia realised Kim was talking to her.

"I don't know." She shrugged. "I don't see what harm it could do."

"That's not what I mean." Kim shook her head, but keeping her eyes on Lydia as she moved to the table to sit next to Lucas.

Lydia gave her a blank stare.

"You seem to be handling this all very well. One minute you are some hotshot in London, living the high life then the next you are told that you aren't who you think you are and your memories have been wiped. There is all this magic, and then there is you and Lucas." She nodded a head in Lucas' direction, who now seemed intrigued by what Kim was saying. "What I am trying to say is that you don't seem fazed by it. Most normal people would be having some type of meltdown but you don't seem bothered."

Lucas raised an eyebrow. A small part of him wanted to know this but the bigger part of him didn't care. He had her back and that was all he cared about.

"Doesn't anything faze you?" Kim raised a quizzical eyebrow as Lydia just sat there drinking her coffee.

"Not really." Lydia replied honestly. She had always been cool, calm and collected.

Kim sighed and rolled her eyes before placing her can down on the counter. This wasn't her plan but she needed to see if she could get a human reaction from Lydia. So as quick as a flash she pulled her top up.

Lydia gasped, spilling her coffee.

"Woah." Lucas covered his eyes and looked away.

"That was the reaction I wanted." Kim pulled her top back down. She was amused by both of their reactions.

Lucas was still looking away as Lydia jumped up to grab a tea towel.

"They were only a pair of tits." Kim gave a heavy sigh, rolled her eyes before picking her can back up.

"There was no need to do that." Lydia was annoyed. Her top was now covered in coffee.

"I needed to check that you were human." Kim pulled a seat out at the table and sat down.

"Of course I am bloody human." Lydia spun around. "If anything I am in shock. Every second I am questioning whether all of this is real." She waved her arms around. "Inside I am screaming but my mind is telling me to be rational and let things play out." Lydia was frustrated and moved to the kitchen door.

"Where're you going?" Lucas asked as he moved to stand up.

"I am going to change my bloody top. You two can stay there and work out what you're supposed to do to bring my memories back."

"Did you have to do that?" Lucas sighed after Lydia had left. The sounds of her feet stomping up the stairs could be heard.

Kim gave an incredulous look as she rolled her eyes then shook her head.

"So..." Kim refused to answer, instead deciding to change the subject. "What's the plan?"

Lucas' eyes had glazed over as he thought about what needed to be done. There needed to be a spell circle and Natalie and Cole needed to be part of it. Natalie was one thing because she had purposely separated herself from the group a long time ago but Cole was a different matter. Lucas just hoped that Cole could put any animosity to one side to help Lydia.

Kim sat there patiently waiting for an answer as she drank from her can. It was almost five minutes before finally Lucas shook his head.

"I need to go and speak to Natalie." He started, leaning forward to lean on the table.

"And you want me to go and speak to Cole?" Kim nodded, taking Lucas by surprise. He hadn't actually thought of that option but right now it seemed perfect.

"Would you?"

Kim shrugged. "It maybe fun to see you all in the room together again and then maybe Lydia can resolve all the tension."

"What tension?" Lydia chose this time to walk back into the kitchen.

She had changed into tight fitting dark jeans and white t-shirt that accentuated her assets perfectly. So perfectly that Lucas' tongue almost fell out of his mouth as his eyes greedily undressed her.

"The tension you caused between the group." Kim got straight to the point without batting an eye.

Lydia flinched.

Lucas' head snapped to Kim. He almost growled at her to back off. Kim had never been one to beat around the bush. She said things how she saw them and refused to lie for anyone.

"Oh come on. You asked for that spell so you could run away from the drama that you were the centre of leaving friction between the rest of us. I think it is about time you got your memories back and faced up to things."

"Back off." Lucas said through gritted teeth.

Lydia shook her head and moved to sit on Lucas' lap in a hope to diffuse the tension. "No. She's right. I need to face up to things. I am older now and hopefully wiser."

Kim gave a smirk mixed with a confused frown. She hadn't expected Lydia to admit her part in all of this so easily but she was also glad that she had helped her admit it.

Lucas, who was still not happy with Kim, wrapped his arms around Lydia's waist and pulled her back against his chest, before burying his head into her neck and trailing soft kisses up to her jaw.

Opposite them Kim made a gagging sound before standing up to place her empty can in the bin.

"Lucas?" Kim turned to look at the pair who seemed to be oblivious to her presence. "Lucas?" She called louder.

This time she got his attention. He didn't stop kissing Lydia's neck but his eyes fluttered open to look at Kim.

"We should go get this over and done with so you two can," she coughed.

Lucas didn't make any moves to leave so she called his name again. This time it was Lydia who prised herself out of Lucas' arms, who groaned a complaint in return.

"I want my memories back. I am sick of being stuck in this rut of not knowing who I am."

"You weren't caring who you were last night." Lucas replied in a low voice, but not low enough because Kim heard.

With a roll of her eyes she shook her head and headed to the door.

"I'll meet you outside." She told him. "And hurry up."

As soon as she left Lucas tried to reach for Lydia but she stepped back.

"All good things come to those who wait." She teased running her eyes down his body before landing on his significant bulge.

Lydia giggled and Lucas looked down before moving his hand to try and adjust himself and after several deep breaths he finally stood up.

He knew more than anything that he needed to get this all arranged, not just because he wanted Lydia to get her memories back but because he planned on spending the next week in bed with her.

"I'll be as quick as I can." He moved to lay a kiss on her forehead. Anything more then he wouldn't be able to stop himself.

"Good luck." Lydia whispered after him.

Chapter Ten

Stepping out of the cottage, Lucas stopped to stare off. From the stone step he could just see over the hedge line and see for miles around. During the summer and spring months everywhere was green. Now all but the fir trees stood bare, their leaves covering the ground in an array of oranges, reds and yellows. The sky was full of lightly greyed clouds and there was a slight cold breeze that nipped at Lucas' nose.

Zipping his coat before stuffing his hands in the front pocket of his jeans, Lucas put one foot in front of the other and slowly made his way towards where Kim was waiting, at the entrance of the driveway.

At first neither of them spoke, as they looked around to see if they were being watched, something they had been taught to do as children.

Satisfied that there was nothing lurking, Lucas finally spoke. "Seven tonight."

Kim nodded. She stood there shivering. On her head she wore a thick, black, woolly hat, paired with a black pair of fingerless gloves. Today she wore light coloured jeans with knee length, black, faux fur lined boots and a black waist length jacket.

"Are you flying?" She asked him as she tried to move around to keep herself warm.

Lucas nodded.

"I'm going to run." She smiled widely.

Lucas chuckled.

Kim had always loved to transform into a black panther believing it to be her spirit animal. Over time she had learned to run just as fast as a panther but in her human form. It was definitely fun to see and it was something Kim enjoyed.

"Have fun." She told him, referring to Natalie.

Kim wasn't one for wishing anyone good luck, believing that you made your own luck but when it came to Natalie she believed all the luck in the world wouldn't get her to break to spell on Lydia. Natalie despised her.

"You too."

"I don't need it. Cole will be more than willing to help. Especially if he thinks he could be in with a chance with Lydia." Kim shrugged and Lucas growled. "Keep your knickers on." She rolled her eyes. "I didn't say it to be true. I have seen the two of you so I know there is no chance," this helped ease Lucas somewhat, "but if we want Cole there then I need to play the cards I am dealt." She winked.

Lucas grunted but said nothing, thinking more about how he would approach Natalie, but he knew that she valued honesty. He just hoped his honesty would be enough to persuade her.

Without another word Lucas watched as Kim took off, jogging at first before picking up speed then disappearing off into the distance.

After a quick glance back at the cottage Lucas took to the sky.

***

"Lucas." Natalie said in surprise as she opened her front door. "Come in." She stepped to one side, allowing Lucas inside.

Natalie stood at five foot four inches with caramel skin, slim figure and brown eyes that looked like pools of milk chocolate. Her brown, curly hair was pulled back tightly into a bun at the back of her head. It had been months since Lucas had seen her and even though she looked good, she also looked tired.

"Hey."

"What brings you here?" She asked, ushering him towards the kitchen.

Natalie's cottage was almost twice the size of Lydia's and whereas once it was busy and loud it was now quiet, apart from the TV in the other room.

"Your parents watching TV?" Lucas asked, not ready to get straight to the point.

"Kind of." Natalie's smile faltered. "Dad is there but sleeping. Mum is with him as she doesn't like it when he is away from her."

"Because that is all she remembers?"

Natalie gave a sad nod. "She thinks I am the hired help."

Lucas' heart went out to her. He had no idea how he would be coping in her situation. All of her siblings had left years ago. They couldn't wait to get out of there and leave Natalie behind to take care of their parents. It infuriated him and he wished he could track each of them down and give them more than a piece of his mind.

"Must be hard." His voice low as he studying her. A big part of him wanted to reach out and hug her but he knew Natalie wouldn't like that. She was always the strong, independent, and resilient one of the group. She hated pity.

Natalie gave a small nod and briefly became lost in her situation before quickly shaking her head and snapping her attention to Lucas. "Out with it."

"Huh?" Lucas pulled a confused face as he tried to act innocent.

"I was born on a day but it wasn't yesterday." She rolled her eyes. "This isn't a social call." Lucas tried to defend himself but Natalie held up a hand. "Cut the crap Lucas. I haven't seen any of you in months-"

"Not our fault. You chose-"

They each cut the other off.

"I know what I chose but I also know that none of you would come to me unless there was something going on. Something you needed me to do." She narrowed her eyes at Lucas as he opened and closed his mouth. Before he could say anything Natalie's face fell before turning to anger. "It's Lydia, isn't it? She's back, isn't she?"

Lucas nodded.

"And what? You have come here to cry on my shoulder?"

"Excuse me Miss?" Just then Natalie's mother appeared in the doorway. She wore a night gown on her frail body. Her dark skin full of wrinkles and her once dark hair was now grey, white and wiry.

"What?" Natalie snapped, making her mother flinch. Quickly Natalie realised what she had done and hurried to her mother. "Everything okay? You should be sitting down." She reached to take her mothers arm and steer her back to the living room but the woman pulled away, looking at Lucas.

"I don't pay you to entertain guests." She spat.

"Of course you don't. He is just leaving." She tried to appease her mother as she tried to steer her out of the room. "Is there anything you need me to get you?" Her voice soothing, bringing her mother's attention from Lucas to herself.

Her mother nodded. "My husband is awake and we would like some dinner." She finally said, allowing Natalie to take her out of the room.

Lucas, who had moved to the doorway of the kitchen, watched as Natalie moved her mother back to the sofa next to where her father's wheelchair sat. In the chair was the almost skeletal frame of a once well built man. In his place was a pale, frail man whose skin was so white that it was practically translucent. He was attached to a ventilator that was hooked to the back of his wheelchair.

Lucas felt sad. Sad for Natalie and sad for her parents.

Once Natalie had placed her mother back on the sofa she checked on her father before saying a few brief words to both of them. When she stood up her eyes briefly locked with Lucas and for a brief moment he saw shame. Shame she should never feel and he wanted to hug her so fiercely.

Taking a deep breath, he stepped back from the doorway and tried to think of all the ways he should be helping Natalie. They were supposed to be friends and even though her siblings had deserted her, her friends shouldn't.

"Just tell me what you came here to say." Natalie said as she waltzed back into the room and started moving to the cupboards to make some food for her parents.

Lucas briefly became lost for words but quickly shook his head.

"Lydia still doesn't have her memories and my parents say we need to do a spell circle."

"And you need someone from the West side?"

Lucas nodded, feeling hopeful. "So you will help?"

"Hell no." She quickly responded without thinking as she continued to make a meal for her parents.

"Natalie..." His voice trailed off as she stopped to stare at him.

"Firstly, my parents need around the clock care and I am the only one to do that. You don't see any of my other family here helping out, do you?" Lucas shook his head and tried to respond but Natalie continued talking. "Secondly, I do not like Lydia so why would I even want to help?"

"Because I asked you to."

"Ha." She said loudly before repeating his words. "Have you ever thought of a job as a comedian?"

"Natalie, please. I know I haven't been here for you but I didn't realise things were this bad. Plus, you hate getting help. But for once I think you are wrong."

Natalie raised her eyebrows as she looked at Lucas in disbelief. "You are going the wrong way to try and persuade me to help you."

"Hear me out." His voice calm as he tried to tread lightly. Maybe he needed to be firmer. "They are your parents and I know you love them very much. I also know that you didn't sign up to take care of them, but you do because you are kind, caring, and selfless. Qualities that make you who you are today but I also think that you deserve at least an hour off, maybe more. I also know that if anyone else in the community knew what your situation was like they would be quick to help you out. So as for getting time off for the spell circle, well, I can guarantee that will be covered. Covered by people that your parents class as friends. Those people who your mother may even remember."

Lucas paused as he watched Natalie's reaction. She was taking everything in but she was also about to speak so he knew he had to continue.

"You are hard headed so do not even think about saying no, because deep down you know that I am right. You are probably mentally and physically exhausted and probably even make different concoctions to keep you going due to lack of sleep." He didn't want to mention that she probably cried herself to sleep. Sometimes things were better left unsaid.

"As for Lydia… you don't like her, big deal. But wouldn't it be better if she knew why instead of wondering who you are and wondering what she has done. I can assure you that she would have no qualms about knocking on your front door and asking you straight out and you wouldn't want that. Wouldn't it be better if she got her memories back and knew exactly what has gone on and why you are so mad at her? Even though I have to say that it isn't her fault."

"She knew I liked Cole." Natalie screeched.

Lucas raised an eyebrow as he looked back at Natalie. "Really? And did he feel the same way about you?"

"That doesn't matter."

Lucas sighed and shook his head but before he could say anything Natalie's mother reappeared.

"Where's my food and who is he?"

"Your food is coming and this is Lucas and he is-"

"Just leaving." Lucas smiled at her mother before looking back at Natalie. "Just think about it. I will send someone over a little before seven. Even if you decide not to come at least allow them to help."

With that Lucas turned and left.

Chapter Eleven

After a quick detour to his parents, Lucas arrived back at the cottage a little after six.

Initially, Lucas felt a sense of calm and warmth that started from somewhere deep within before spreading to his outer most extremities at being in such close proximity to Lydia. That quickly changed at the sound of Cole's deep voice met with the distinctive laughter of Lydia causing the hairs of the back of his neck to bristle.

Closing the front door, Lucas stepped into the kitchen.

"Cole."

"Lucas."

They both said the other's name with a swift nod of the head whilst wearing the same stony expression.

At seeing Lucas, Lydia's face lit up and she moved from where she sat at the kitchen table with both Cole and Kim to go to Lucas.

"How did it go?" Her eyes solely on him as Lucas saw Cole watching the pair of them interact through narrowed eyes until Kim tapped Cole's arm to distract him.

"Okay, I think." He sighed and in return Lydia raised a confused eyebrow. "She has a lot going on but I got my mother involved and hopefully she will be able to persuade her."

Lydia looked disappointed as she gave a small nod.

"In the meantime," he started before looking towards Kim. "How about we set this place up."

"On it." Kim called out and jumped up from the table.

Within minutes Kim, with the help of Cole, managed to clear and move the table, along with the rug that was situated directly underneath to reveal a large circular metal plate. It looked more like an oversized man hole cover but with lots of weird symbols and writing in a language Lydia did not know.

As Lydia kept back out of the way, she watched as Lucas produced a block of chalk from his jacket pocket before drawing a larger circle, two feet further out than the metal plate but putting it slap bang in the middle. Next he wrote the marks of a compass as Kim and Cole began to place candles around the kitchen.

When they were done there were a couple of minutes until seven and there was still no sign of Natalie.

"You did tell her the correct time, right?" Kim said with mild irritation. It wasn't lost on Lydia that Kim seemed to have a dislike for Natalie.

"Of course I did." Lucas himself was beginning to feel frustrated. Natalie may not like Lydia but he had gone out of his way to offer her help, the least she could do was show him some respect, even if it was to send message that she wasn't coming.

All the time Lydia said nothing as she nervously chewed the inside of her mouth, worrying about what would happen. Would it hurt? How quick would the memories come back?

"Worried?" Cole asked as he sidled up beside her and leaned against the kitchen counter to give Lydia a flirtatious lopsided smile.

Lydia nodded. "A little." She felt sick as the nerves ate away at her insides. It was only light tapping at the front door that had her head snapping in that direction as Cole muttered his annoyance under his breath.

"She's here." Lucas said as he hurried to the door.

"About bloody time." Kim glowered.

"Sorry it took longer than expected to walk your parents through everything." Natalie said as Lucas opened the door and invited her inside.

"Thank you for coming." He told her gratefully.

"Yeah well... I just want to get this over and done with so I can go home." She retorted before glancing into the kitchen. Her eyes swooping across Cole, Kim and Lydia who were standing side by side.

"Let's begin then shall we." Cole rubbed his hands together with a wide smile.

"Hi, I'm-"

"I know exactly who you are." Natalie cut Lydia off. "I haven't come here for any idle chitchat or to pretend we are all bosom buddies." Natalie ensured that she met eyes with everyone. "I am here for one thing and one thing only. When the spell has been lifted I will go and you don't have to worry about seeing or hearing from me again." She gave them a bored expression as she shrugged herself out of her coat and placed it on the table that had been pushed into the far corner before moving to stand on the west point of the circle.

"Frosty." Kim muttered before moving to stand on the east point and glaring at Natalie who refused to make eye contact with her. Instead Natalie chose to look at the central point of the metal plate.

"What do I do?" Lydia asked nervously.

Cole was about to place a hand on the small of her back and give her instruction when Lucas quickly jumped in and steered Lydia to the centre of the circle. He placed her so that she was facing him.

"You move around the circle in a clockwise position until you are facing the person you feel drawn to. Once done, we will begin chanting. If it works, then move anti-clockwise for 360 degrees."

"Huh?" Lydia pulled a confused face making Lucas chuckle.

"Move around the circle clockwise until you face the person you are most drawn to." He said with encouragement and she stood there facing him. "And when you are happy with your choice raise your hand so we can begin."

Lucas expected Lydia to raise her hand but instead she gave a small nod and moved to face Kim who smirked in Lucas' direction. Within seconds though the smirk was gone as Lydia turned to face Cole. A smug expression slowly spreading across his face as Lydia remained facing him.

Lucas was not happy and he was about to ask Lydia if that was her choice when she turned again. This time it took seconds for her to raise her hand as she looked directly at Natalie who stared back at her.

Natalie said or did anything. Her face showed no expression as she acted as though Lydia was not there and stared right through her.

Lucas nodded in surprise before glancing at everyone else to ensure that they were ready. Each of them gave a brief nod, without even glancing at Lucas.

Taking a deep breath Lucas began to chant in a language Lydia had never heard. She almost jumped when the other three joined in. Together they almost sounded like a didgeridoo.

As they chanted Lydia felt as though her mind was being pulled. She closed her eyes to try and block out the intense pressure. Swirls of colours splattered across her mind and image after image filled her head until finally the chanting stopped.

No one said a word.

Everything was silent as they waited with bated breath to see if it had worked.

Suddenly Lydia's eyes flew open, causing Natalie to gasp with fright. Lydia's face was blank as she stared directly at Natalie before finally taking a deep breath.

"You and I were best friends but you were upset when Cole chose me as the object of his affections when it was you who so badly wanted them."

Natalie blushed and briefly glanced at Cole as Lydia continued.

"I never asked for it to happen the way it did and I didn't want to lose you as a friend. We are older now and much wiser. I hope that you can overcome your animosity towards me so that we can continue as friends. I thank you for helping me unlock my mind."

Just those words had everyone collectively sighing a huge sigh of relief. It had worked.

Lydia turned to face Cole who gave a wide smile.

Lydia's face was still expressionless as she focused on what to say.

"Our relationship was based on a lie." She began and Kim sniggered at the words as Cole looked as though he had been slapped in the face. "At first I was a game to you. A toy, you might say. You knew Lucas had feelings for me and decided it would be fun to get in there before him. The problem was, you used a spell to get me into that relationship so my feelings for you were never real. Yours, however, were. The Gods are angry with what you have done and warn that there will be dire consequences if you do something like that again."

Cole gulped as every eye focused on him. The others hadn't realised it was a spell he had used but hearing Lydia say that made everything become much clearer.

"I thank you for helping me unlock my mind." She finally nodded before turning to look at Kim. This time a small smile played at the corner of Lydia's lips.

"Well, well, well. If it isn't the most honest person of the bunch."

Lydia was met with a nervous stare. She could have so much fun at Kim's expense like she does with so many others.

"Through my entire life you have always been the comedienne. The first one there when someone is feeling down. You are a great friend and a great ally. The Gods know your secrets and know that you aren't as honest as you say you are."

Lydia could have continued and told all of Kim's secrets but she knew that it wasn't her place to say. She would leave that to Kim herself.

"I thank you for helping me unlock my mind." She nodded before taking a deep breath and turning to look at Lucas, who was still frowning in Kim's direction as he tried to figure out her secrets were. Lydia was thankful that whilst in this circle there was no way Lucas could read her thoughts. She was also thankful that with the unlocking of her mind came the unlocking of all of her powers, and some she could not wait to try out.

"Lucas…" His name almost a whisper on her tongue. "My entire life you have been my rock. Even when I was in a relationship with Cole you still chose to be my best friend and putting your feelings to one side. You have always been the quieter one of the group, preferring to speak through actions instead of words."

Colour rose in Lydia's cheeks and Lucas gave a toothy smile knowing exactly what she was referring to.

"You are my rock, my heart, my spirit, my best friend, and my soulmate. I thank you for never giving up on me and showering me with your love and affection." Her smile growing wider. "I thank you for helping me unlock my mind."

With that the spell circle ended, and as Lucas rushed to cup Lydia's face in his hands before gently placing a kiss on her lips.

"You remember everything?" He asked, not wanting to get ahead of himself.

Lydia nodded as she wrapped her arms around his waist. "Everything. And we have a lot of making up to do." She spoke between kisses. "And I need to get a divorce."

The sound of someone clearing their throat had them both reluctantly tearing their eyes away to look at Kim. Quickly glancing around they noticed that both Cole and Natalie had already left.

"I don't think either of them wanted to stick around for pleasantries." Kim smirked.

"You may want to leave too." Lucas told her, receiving a playful swat on his arm from Lydia. "What? We are about to set this cottage on fire. So unless she wants to catch fire…" His voice trailed off as he lifted Lydia and wrapped her legs around his waist.

Lydia giggled and Kim rolled her eyes as she headed to the door as Lucas carried Lydia to the stairs.

"Lydia?" Kim paused in the doorway, stopping Lucas as he made it to the second step.

"Don't worry, your secrets are safe." She winked.

"What secrets?" Lucas flicked his head back and forth between Kim and Lydia.

"Never you mind." Lydia rolled her eyes before seeing Kim give her an appreciative smile as she left the cottage.

Chapter Twelve

Eleven days the cottage blazed like an inferno as Lucas and Lydia made love, barely stopping for a couple of hours sleep in between. Neither of them could get enough of the other. They were each other's salvation. Their means to stay alive.

With each time their bodies united as one a new tattoo appeared until they were almost covered from head to toe. Each of them knowing that they could mask the tattoos from others if they needed to.

It was late Sunday evening and Lucas had Lydia's legs wrapped around his waist as he pressed her against one of the bookcases in the living room as he drove home his passion to her very core. Both of them panting as they held tightly to each other. Lydia's nails digging deep into Lucas' back as they both climaxed.

Only when Lucas had fully released did he walk over towards the sofa before gently lowering Lydia, moving himself down with her.

"I want to go to London." Lydia finally said through pants as Lucas placed his hands on the arm of the sofa to hold himself slightly up so as not to squash her. "I think it is time to close that chapter in my life once and for all."

"I agree."

"I think we should drive down in the morning."

"Drive?" Lucas raised an eyebrow. Now that Lydia had her powers back she could also transform into any animal and he was sure there would be something they could both transform into that would be better than driving.

"Yes." Lydia gave a wicked smile. "I have an idea."

Lucas' eyes were heavy as he lowered his head so their lips were almost touching. "Well how about you tell me with your mind because your mouth has better things to do." He told her before hungrily pressing his lips on hers.

Each time they kissed felt even better than the last. Their bodies pined for the other. Neither of them feeling sore or exhausted from all of the love making. They didn't want to stop, loving the feeling of being so close.

Lydia's back arched and she let out a moan as Lucas pushed deep inside her, making her momentarily forget her idea as she allowed her body to be taken over with euphoric pleasure.

***

It was a little after seven in the morning when Lydia slowly began to awake from her slumber. With a large smile on her face she stretched and yawned before slowly opening her eyes. She was back in her own bed but alone. Briefly closing her eyes, she allowed her mind to search for Lucas until she found him in his parent's kitchen.

Make sure you bring some of your father's baking back with you. I'm starving. She whispered into his mind only to be met with Lucas chuckling.

I will do.

With that Lydia smiled and pulled back from his mind. Her powers were definitely strong and she had never felt more alive. Those years she spent in London were nothing more than a blip. Something she would rather quickly be done with before locking it away in the farthest reaches of her mind.

Lydia was about to head downstairs to wait for Lucas so that they could start the long journey down to London when she felt a pull towards her parent's bedroom. She hadn't been in there since that first time but smiled when she opened the bedroom door to see the room filled with vibrant colours.

The cottage was no longer in mourning and Lydia felt herself reaching out to stroke at the caramel coloured wallpaper.

"Good girl." She whispered to the cottage.

Since regaining her memories, along with her powers, Lydia felt an overwhelming special bond to the cottage. It was as though it were family. A sister or a great aunt. Something or someone who looked out for her. Who would protect her without a single hesitation. It felt her emotions. When she was sad, so was the cottage. So in that theory, it was also an extension of herself.

A calmness enveloped her as though the cottage were wrapping invisible arms of comfort around her as she moved into the room, ready to be there for her if the tears came.

"I'm okay." She reassured the cottage as she moved to sit on the bed.

After a quick glance and smile at the picture of her parents, who she knew were somewhere close by in spirit, Lydia opened the boxes on the bed and ran her hands over the Christmas decorations. All of them were handmade including some she had made as a child.

"I'm going to be gone for a few days." She told the cottage, without looking up from the decorations. "I won't object if you decide to start hanging up the decorations." She smiled as she lifted a reindeer made from twigs. "Lucas can get us a lovely tree, when we get back."

The cottage creaked in a form of acknowledgement.

Closing the box back up, Lydia walked back to the wall and placed a hand, this time moving closer so her head almost touched.

"I promise to hurry back. I won't ever leave you again." She whispered gently before placing a light kiss on the wall.

The cottage sounded as though it sighed. Lydia knew it was happy. She could feel it inside her.

With a final smile she left her parents bedroom, closing the door behind her, before heading downstairs.

She had just reached the bottom step when Lucas opened the door wearing a huge smile as he held up a bag.

Lydia didn't need to be told what was it in, she could smell the assortment of cakes, cookies and bread.

Giving Lucas a quick kiss she reached her hand inside the bag and pulled out a triple chocolate chip cookie before taking a bite. Closing her eyes, she made sounds of approval.

"I think we best get going." Lucas spoke causing Lydia to open her eyes. "That cookie is making me jealous."

Lydia laughed and pushed the rest of her cookie into her mouth, filling it completely.

Lucas laughed and shook his head before turning to open the door as Lydia skipped out to the car.

***

It was late when they finally arrived in London so they checked into a hotel and called Mr Langford. He had assured Lydia that he would take care of the car and have it dropped off outside of the home she had shared with Steve.

Mr Langford had already drafted up the divorce papers and would be meeting Lydia and Lucas outside her old home at 12:30pm.

In the morning Lydia planned on going to the company that employed her and handing in her notice.

"No touching." Lydia warned Lucas as she climbed into bed.

It was difficult to keep their hands off each other without ending up naked. Normally that would have been great but they were staying in a hotel and Lydia didn't want to imagine what would happen to the building as a result of them getting a bit heated.

Lucas stuck out his bottom lip and pretended to sulk. Yes, he was slightly disappointed but he had had the exact same thoughts.

He had heard stories of other soul mates setting fire to forests and various buildings that weren't connected to them.

The cottage was very much connected to them. He knew that the cottage felt every single touch he placed on Lydia. To normal people this would be weird, but as part warlock Lucas was well aware of his connection to elements as well as natural objects. The cottage was very much a natural object, made by Lydia's ancestors. The cottage would always be connected to her and her family, and by extension himself.

He felt as though Lydia was a fire and he was air. On its own, the fire could be controlled but the two of them together took things to the highest levels imaginable. At least in the cottage it could be maintained. Outside of the cottage... Lucas didn't want to think about it.

Another thing he didn't want to think about was Steve. On the one hand, Lucas could not wait until tomorrow was over but on the other he wanted to beat the crap out of Steve. Not only for hurting Lydia but also for jealous reasons.

Steve may not have been Lydia's first kiss but she was the first person she was intimate with and the first person she had married, when Lucas knew that if she had her memories back it would never would have happened, which only infuriated him even more.

He needed to get tomorrow out of the way then, hopefully, they could both forget all about this blip in her life.

Chapter Thirteen

It was dark when Lydia awoke. Lucas was lightly snoring beside her. Careful not to wake him, Lydia quietly slipped out of bed and out of the bedroom.

She was glad she spent the extra money for this hotel room. It may not have been a Penthouse Suite but it was close enough with a large bedroom, bathroom and its own kitchen and living room.

After grabbing a mug of coffee, Lydia moved to stand at one of the windows. As far as her eyes could see, everywhere was lit up with twinkling lights. Down below vehicles and people still moved around. It was one of those cities that never sleeps. At one time Lydia loved it but now… things were different.

Now that her memories were back she had questioned why, a lot. London was so different than the reality of Mystic Valley that she wondered why she had chosen to live here. Her head throbbed from all of the noise and smog. Then there was the money she had made here. To some it may not have been a lot but to Lydia it was much more than she would ever need. If anything, she couldn't imagine ever needing the money, because she planned to never leave Mystic Valley again.

Lydia had no idea how long she had been standing there, but it was long enough that the sun and noise outside was just rising.

Today was going to be a good day. It would close the door on something she didn't want to revisit and open another door to her future.

Turning around Lydia smiled as a sleepy Lucas opened the bedroom door with a yawn.

He was her future and she was grateful that he was here today.

Yes, today was definitely going to be a great day.

***

Mystic Valley series

It was just after nine in the morning when Lydia, accompanied by Lucas, made her way up to the top floor of the building where she used to work. This was the floor which housed the director's offices and when they stepped out of the lift they stepped onto pristine, white, tiled, floor.

The whole floor was shaped like a three leafed clover. Each leaf was an office of each of the three directors. Outside of their offices sat their secretaries, but before you could even get to them there was a reception desk right in the centre. It was black and raised so the receptionist sat three feet above the ground. Lydia always wondered how the receptionist got to her chair. Did she have to climb a ladder? Lydia couldn't tell because the desk was enclosed in black paneling that surrounded the desk in a circle.

The receptionist was the gatekeeper to these directors and it was up to her if she allowed you to cross the threshold and see them. Even if she did you would have to contend with the director's secretaries next.

Luckily for Lydia she was well known after becoming the youngest senior marketing executive in the company. She even had the passcode for the lift that brought her to this floor. Normally it would stop the floor below.

Today the receptionist was Louise. A fresh faced woman in her thirties who looked to have spent a lot of time having plastic surgery. On the outside she looked like a stereotypical airhead with all of her makeup, big puffy blonde hair, huge breasts and tight fitting clothes. But that was just a disguise to the ruthlessness.

Louise was good at her job. No one ever got to see the directors without an appointment. If your name was not on the list, then you weren't getting in and Louise would tell you where to go wearing the sweetest of smiles. That woman could kill you with kindness.

The company was male dominated so they normally flustered around Louise, but not Lydia.

"Good morning." Lydia smiled as she walked towards the desk.

At first Louise said nothing as her eyes narrowed first on Lydia before lingering a little too long on Lucas. Not that he noticed but Lydia surely did.

"Good morning." Louise's head snapped back to Lydia with a huge smile, revealing her pearly white veneers. "Do you have an appointment?" She fixed Lydia with a penetrating stare as her smile grew wider. She was like a venomous snake ready to bite.

"Actually I don't-" Lydia started to say but was quickly cut off.

"I am sorry the Directors are very busy today and unless you have an appointment then you will not be able to see them." The smile never wavering from her face.

"Mr Montgomery will definitely want to see me today."

"I am sure that if he did then you would have an appointment."

Lydia sighed and rolled her eyes. "Listen Louise." Lydia tilted her head to one side and smiled. "May I call you Louise?" Louise blinked in response but said nothing. "If you do not allow me to see Mr Montgomery and he discovers that I was here, then I am 100% certain that you will lose your job, then how will you get the money to pay for all of your surgery? Because you won't be able to blow the bosses any more."

Louise's face turned red. She was furious.

Slamming her hands on the desk she stood up, making her over ten feet tall. Lydia wasn't intimidated as she smiled up at Louise.

"I'll show myself then?" Lydia didn't even wait for a response as she started heading towards Mr Montgomery's secretary as Louise began to rant.

"You can't go in there." She shouted as she lifted up the phone. "I am calling security."

"Go for it. I am sure it will be to escort you off the premises." Lydia winked before hurrying towards the secretary.

She was winging it. She wanted to at least get to see the secretary before security did arrive. Luckily for Lydia, Mr Montgomery was standing at his secretary's desk and looked up as Lydia and Lucas hurried in his direction.

"Lydia?" He gave a puzzled expression and took in her appearance. He had never seen Lydia in anything but a suit and here she was wearing jeans, t-shirt and a short leather jacket. He didn't like it. He expected his employees to dress smartly. In fact, he expected everyone to dress smartly and to make matters worse he saw that she was with a man that was dressed in similar type of clothing, expect Lucas' jeans had rips in them and he wore scuffed boots that weren't tied up properly.

"Mr Montgomery, I need to speak with you." Lydia glanced behind her to make sure Louise or security weren't coming after her. They weren't but she could hear the lift doors pinging.

Mr Montgomery looked from Lydia to Lucas back to Lydia before glancing at two burly security guards who looked hungry for action.

Before the two security guards could say anything Mr Montgomery waved his arm to try and shoo them away. "Do you not realise who this is?" The security guards responded with blank stares. "This is Lydia Green and she is the senior marketing executive of this company."

At first the security guards looked confused and then disappointed but then they turned their attention to Lucas.

"He's with me." Lydia was quick to respond.

Mr Montgomery glanced at Lucas before back at the security guards. "You are not needed here." He told them before turning his attention back to Lydia. "Your friend can wait out here." He finally said before turning to walk back into his office where he held the door open.

At first Lydia just stood there wondering what to do before turning back to Lucas. "I won't be long." She told him.

Lucas nodded and watched as Lydia walked into her boss's office. Once the door closed Lucas stood there looking around. Everything was so white. Too white. There were various art pieces hung on the walls but to Lucas it looked more liked something had thrown up on the canvas.

"You can sit over here." A voice said from behind.

Lucas turned to see an older woman looking at him nervously before seeing where she was pointing.

Ten feet from her desk were marble stones which had been made into seats. It was supposed to be an art piece but to Lucas it looked hideous and when he sat down on one he spent his time adjusting as it was so uncomfortable.

In Mr Montgomery's office Lydia had just finished explaining to him that she was moving back home so would not be coming back to work for the company. She had expected him to be furious but for a long while he remained silent.

Lydia said nothing more though as she waited for Mr Montgomery to digest what she had just told him. She hadn't gone into too much detail. She had told him that her parents had died and there was no one to run the family business.

"Are you sure this is what you want to do?" He finally spoke. "You know; you don't have to run the family business. You can employ someone or sell the company or-"

"No, I want to." She interrupted. "I forgot how much I had missed home until I was there."

Mr Montgomery nodded before sucking in his lips and drumming his fingers on the table. "You know this leaves me in a huge dilemma. The Christmas ad has gone out and we are working on the sales one which means that we really need your expertise."

"I understand and I do have a recommendation."

Mr Montgomery stopped drumming his fingers. "I'm listening."

Lydia smiled widely. This was her first plan of action.

Mystic Valley series

***

Lydia left the office smiling. Mr Montgomery had even given her a hug and wished her well in her future endeavours, and after leaving him a forwarding address, which was Mr Langford's, Lydia had a skip in her step.

"Ready?" Lucas asked as he stood.

"I need to speak to someone before we leave." She told him, ignoring Louise's evil glare as they stepped into the lift and headed down to the marketing floor.

Stepping out onto the marketing floor was completely different from the Director's floor. This one was carpeted in a deep brown colour. The walls were beige and the smell of coffee permeated the air. It may have been chaos with people hurrying around but it was a place that Lydia had called home. It was friendly. Everyone knew everyone's name. Some may have been running around but there was a feeling of happiness and hunger. A hunger to be successful. To make the best marketing advert possible knowing that it was a clear representation of the employees themselves.

Lydia had loved it here. But now… now the chaos was overwhelming.

People stopped to look in Lydia and Lucas' direction. Some waved and smiled. Others called out her name. She may have been someone they had call boss but she had also been their friend.

Lydia smiled and waved back as she moved through the throngs of people to her office where a new secretary sat outside.

Lydia smiled but said nothing as she moved to open the door. The secretary began to panic. Jumping up and telling Lydia that she couldn't just walk in there but then she heard Audrey.

"Lydia." She practically squealed as barreled into Lydia, wrapping her arms tightly around her before holding her out at arm's length. "Look at you." She gushed. "You look amazing. How are you?"

Lydia nodded as behind her Lucas shut the door and stood there awkwardly.

"I am great." Lydia replied honestly as Audrey released her and gave Lucas an approving look. "This is Lucas. My better half." She smiled – it growing when Audrey looked at them both in confusion.

"Hi." Lucas held out his hand and Audrey happily took it. "Lydia obviously has it wrong. I am the lucky one here."

Audrey looked back and forth, still completely confused.

Lydia gave a small laugh before telling Audrey about catching Steve and Mandy together and how Lucas was her first love and how they got back together when she went home.

"Oh my." Audrey explained as she moved around to the chair that Lydia had once sat in. "If you don't mind me saying…" She looked to Lydia for permission to continue and Lydia nodded. "I never liked Steve anyway. He seemed slimy."

Lydia shrugged. "Yeah. I realise that now." She sighed but wished she had found out sooner.

"Soooo…" Audrey over exaggerated. "When are you coming back?"

"I'm not." Lydia smiled with a shrug.

"What? No. Who is going to run this place?" She exclaimed.

"You."

"Me?" Audrey shook her head in disbelief. "I can't. Plus, the Directors-"

"I have just spoken to Mr Montgomery and it has all been arranged. He is happy with the work you have been doing in my absence and I helped him see that you are the only person suitable for this role."

Audrey paled. She shook her head in disbelief.

Lydia took this opportunity to move around to the other side of the table and kneel before Audrey.

"You have worked for this company for decades. You know most of the core factors of every single department but your passion has always been marketing which was why you came to me. For years you have been overlooked and you have doubted your self-worth. You are a major asset to this company and I know that when I leave here I am leaving with the knowledge that this department is in safe hands."

Tears sparkled in Audrey's eyes. This was her dream. She had applied to work in this department a long time ago but was rejected, which is why she took on the role as the secretary to the directors. Back then they only needed one secretary. But as the company grew so did Audrey's knowledge. She asked to be transferred to marketing. If she couldn't work on advertising she could work alongside those who did.

In the past few weeks Audrey had thrived. She believed Lydia would be back so she ensured that Lydia would not come back to a mess. But now…

"Think of it as an early Christmas present." Lydia winked and stood up. Moving to Lucas before they moved towards the door.

Just before they left Audrey found her voice and stood up.

"Thank you." She managed to say.

Lydia nodded. "You are the one person I will miss."

"I'll miss you too." Audrey was able to mumble as Lydia and Lucas left.

Chapter Fourteen

Lydia and Lucas arrived outside the block of apartments, where Lydia had once lived with Steve, a few minutes before Mr Langford.

"You used to live here?" Lucas tried not to say it in disgust but it was hard not to. He was surrounded by lots of tall, bricked, buildings without any trees in sight and lots of vehicles parked on either side of the street.

At one point Lydia had looked at this place as an amazing location, but now… it looked hideous and very over crowded.

"I would tell you that it looks better inside and I wouldn't be completely lying."

"You can't polish shit." Lucas said, looking up and around.

Lydia laughed. Yeah, she had to agree. You could put all sorts of glitter, ribbon and sparkles on a pile of shit but at the end of the day it was still a pile of shit.

"Oh there you are." Mr Langford suddenly appeared, making Lydia look around as she tried to figure out from where. but he was small. He barely reached her hip and he was carrying a briefcase whilst wearing a trench coat and a bowler hat.

Lydia tried to stifle a giggle but it was hard not to laugh. The outfit looked odd on him. Not only that, she didn't even know that they made adult clothes that small.

"We got here early." Lucas told him, giving Lydia a warning side-glance. He had read her mind. Lydia was definitely back to her normal self. She had always liked teasing Mr Langford, from as far back as he could remember.

"Yes…well… I have been trying to find the car park space." He flustered, waving his free arm.

"It's just around the back. I'll show you." Lydia led the way to the private car park. Luckily she still had the keys to it.

No sooner had she unlocked it than she heard the sound of a large truck reversing.

Turning around Lydia smiled widely and stood back as two men helped unload the car and put it in Steve's driving space before getting their paperwork signed.

Neither the driver or his co-worker asked any questions, probably used to things like this happening, before they drove away leaving Lydia standing there smiling widely.

In the driving space was Steve's most prized possession, only now it was nicely crushed into a rectangle.

"Excellent." Lucas laughed, even more so when Lydia clicked a button on the set of keys and it beeped and a light flashed.

"Steve will think twice about cheating on anyone again." Lydia winked as she locked the gates before the three of them walked into the building.

"I have all of your paperwork ready. All Steve needs to do is sign it. Once he has done I will get it filed and as soon as it is finalised I will bring them straight up to you." Mr Langford stated as the moved towards the lift.

Lydia had a feeling that there was no way that Mr Langford could walk all the way to the top of the building. It would be like climbing a mountain.

The lift stopped on the floor below their destination. None of them said anything as they made their way up to the apartment.

Standing outside Lydia began to feel nervous. Lucas placed a gentle hand on her back to try and calm her nerves and after one final breath Lydia unlocked the door.

She gasped.

Her once pristine home was a mess. There were clothes, beer bottles, pizza bottles and so much more strewn across the place and sat amongst it all was Steve who quickly jumped up when he heard the door open.

He looked as though he hadn't shaved for a few days. Something told Lydia though that it was all for her benefit. Steve wanted to play the victim card. He wanted to show her that he had been distraught without her and that he had been so worried. She knew it was bullshit because Mr Langford had had people watching him.

There had been parties and there had been more than Mandy he had been bringing back here. He did wonder if Mandy was aware of this.

"Lydia." Steve fake gasped before frowning as he looked first at Lucas and then at Mr Langford. "Who are you?" A note of anger in his voice.

"This is my friend from home." Lydia had decided not to give too much away about her and Lucas' relationship in case Steve tried to play on it and argue the divorce. "And this is my solicitor, Mr Langford."

"Solicitor?" Steve frowned as he watched as the small man in the trench coat take off his bowler hat as he moved around to the front of the sofa where Steve stood before clearing a space on the coffee table. It was so cluttered that Mr Langford just used his briefcase to push everything onto the floor before laying his briefcase down.

"I am representing Mrs Green with her divorce."

"Divorce?" Steve asked in surprise as he looked from Mr Langford to Lydia.

"You sound surprised." Lydia raised a questioning eyebrow as she moved to stand at the side of the sofa.

Steve opened and closed his mouth then rubbed at his head. "You disappear. I think you are dead. Your secretary tells me that your parents died." Steve lifted and dropped his arms. "I didn't even know you had any parents."

"Everyone has parents." Lucas interjected from where he stood at the front door with his arms closed.

Steve's head snapped in his direction and his eyes narrowed.

"Is he who you are divorcing me for? Were you cheating on me with him?" He spat, pointing a finger at Lucas.

Lucas scoffed as he glowered at Steve. He was still trying to wrap his head around what she had ever seen in him. He was a scrawny little rat. How the heck he managed to get Lydia to marry him was beyond him.

"You've got no room to talk." Lydia told Steve in a clipped tone.

His anger quickly gave way to innocence. "I don't know what you mean."

"The day I discovered my parents died was the same day I caught you and Mandy upstairs in the hot tub." Lydia's voice rising. "How long have the two of you been together? Was it going on before we even got together? You know what? I don't even care. You and me are over. I want you to sign the divorce papers so I can get you out of my life for good."

Steve reeled. He thought he had been discreet. She knew and he needed to cover it up.

"It was one time. It was a mistake. It never happened again and it won't. I promise. Please." He begged.

At the moment Mr Langford lifted up a photograph which caught everyone's attention. It was of Steve and Mandy being intimate.

Looking down at the table they all saw that Mr Langford had several photographs laid out on top of his briefcase. Each one clearly showing Steve being unfaithful.

Steve's face twisted in anger.

"You've been spying on me?" He snarled as he began tearing at the pictures before making a move towards Mr Langford, but Lucas reacted quickly and jumped the sofa and grabbing Steve by the shirt before shoving him back until he slammed against the wall.

"Easy man." Steve raised his hands in apology but Lucas said nothing as Mr Langford and Lydia walked forward.

Steve knew he was no match for Lucas so he wasn't even going to try and fight him off.

"Here is how this is going to play out." Lucas started to say. "You are going to listen to everything Lydia and Mr Langford have to say. You will also kindly accept the offer they are about to give you. If you don't then I have no problem in beating the living day lights out of you."

Steve blinked, then blinked some more hoping that this was just a dream.

"Do I make myself clear?" Lucas pulled at Steve before slamming him back against the wall. This time harder.

"Yes." Steve painfully squeaked.

"Good." Lucas dropped him and stepped back.

"I brought your car back." Lydia dangled the keys as though they were a carrot and Steve were the horse.

He made a move to grab them but Lydia quickly put them away.

"You sign the divorce papers and you get the keys."

Steve narrowed his eyes as he ground his jaw it was only when Lucas took a step forward did he jump and speak. "Where do I sign?"

Both Lucas and Lydia smiled.

"I need to explain a few things first." Mr Langford spoke. "My client, Mrs Green, is willing to sign both the car and apartment over to you. She is also willing to cover the mortgage for the next six months. After that you are on your own. She will no longer financially support you. Is that understood?"

Steve looked at Mr Langford and he had to admit that it was a better offer than he expected. He would have liked more but he knew there was no way.

Steve nodded.

"Good. Now, I need you to sign here and here to say that you agree to the terms. Then I need you both to sign here and here."

Both Lydia and Steve nodded.

This was it. Lydia smiled nervously. She held her breath until Steve signed everything before she finally signed her name.

Mystic Valley series

"That's that then. Your papers will be in the post once it is finalised."

"Keys." Steve held out a hand, palm up, and made a grabbing action.

Lydia stepped forward and dropped the keys in his hand.

No sooner had she done so did Steve quickly hurry out of the apartment.

"Let's go on the roof and see if we can see him." Lydia suggested, making her way to the steps before hurrying up them.

Behind her Lydia heard a grunt before turning around to see Lucas carrying Mr Langford up the stairs.

"Put me down." He demanded and Lucas obliged but only once they had made it to the top.

Whilst Mr Langford patted himself down, ensuring that his coat was not creased, Lucas hurried to the edge of the apartment block and peered over the edge just as Steve ran into the car park.

At first Steve just stood there, looking around before it dawned on him that the piled of scrap metal was in fact his car. As soon as the reality of what was in front of him hit him, he let out a string of expletives before kicking the metal and howling out in pain. Only they never heard his cries as the car alarm started going off.

Lydia and Lucas erupted in laughter before stepping back.

"I think I want to go home." Lydia told Lucas.

Lucas nodded and started to walk towards the stairs but Lydia grabbed his hand and shook her head. Lucas gave her a confused look.

"I want to fly."

His eyes grew wide as he looked at her. It had been years since Lydia had transformed into anything. "Are you sure?"

Lydia nodded before turning to thank Mr Langford.

"Wait." Mr Langford held onto Lydia's hand. "Almost eight years ago your parents entrusted me with you. I was your guardian and it was my job to watch over you from a far. Before bringing you here they cast a spell, a spell in which you would be lucky in everything you do."

"Which was why I got the job I wanted?"

Mr Langford nodded. "Though I have no idea why you ended up with that cretin." He tutted and rolled his eyes.

Lydia laughed. "Me either."

"I will ensure that I will bring everything to you in one piece, as well as your clothes." Mr Langford nodded towards the clothes she was wearing.

It took a few moments before Lydia realised that once she transformed into an eagle her clothes would be left here on the floor.

"Thank you." She told Mr Langford before taking him by complete surprise and hugging him.

Whilst Mr Langford regained his composure – he wasn't a man who liked physical contact – Lydia moved to where Lucas stood.

"Ready?" He asked and Lydia gave an excited nod before they both transformed into eagles and flew in the direction of home.

Lydia was done with London. Her final and only destination was Mystic Valley.

The End

About Author

Lavinia grew up in a small town in Cheshire, England, before moving to Scotland in 2000. She now lives just outside Edinburgh with her husband Ian and their two daughters Erin and Kasey-ray.

Lavinia has been writing since an early age, something that both her children have inherited. She started by writing poetry, one of which was turned into lyrics for a song. By the age of 14, Lavinia had written 7 books in an unpublished series.

After moving to Scotland she stopped writing for a while, it was only after writing a short story for her eldest daughter's school about anti-bullying and how you should stay in school and learn, that Lavinia felt the yearning to write again, this was also helped by her eldest daughter and her thirst for literature when she asked her mother to write her another story. This was how this book series came about.

Mystic Valley series

Where to find out more

www.laviniaurban.co.uk

www.facebook.com/LaviniaUrbanAuthor

www.facebook.com/groups/LaviniasUrbanLegends

laviniaurban.blogspot.co.uk/

twitter.com/Lavinia_Missb

Lavinia is also available on Instagram, Pinterest and much more.

Made in the USA
Charleston, SC
28 February 2017